ADVANCE PRAISE FOR *BINGO BARGE MURDER*

"A solid first entry in the Shay O'Hanlon mystery series. Chandler writes with a wonderful sense of place, plenty of humor, and a crisp pace. The best part for me was the characters, which were so richly drawn that they felt like instant friends. This is a great read from the very first page!"

—Ellen Hart, award-winning author of the Jane Lawless series and the Sophie Greenway series

"Chandler's debut is fast and funny ... crammed with memorably quirky Minnesota characters."

—Brian Freeman, bestselling author of *Immoral*

"Jessie Chandler delivers a fresh murder motive in this engaging debut mystery."

—Julie Kramer, author of *Stalking Susan*

"What do you get if you line up Shay O'Hanlon, owner of a café called the Rabbit Hole, a scrumptious police detective named JT Bordeaux, a computer genius drama queen, and a murder at the Pig's Eye Bingo Barge? If you said a rollicking, fast-paced blackout game of mystery and suspense, I'd have to yell 'BINGO!'"

—Mary Logue, author of *Frozen Stiff*

"If anything happens to me, I want Shay O'Hanlon on my side! *Bingo Barge Murder* is a fun read with an emotional depth that sneaks up on you. The characters are interesting and quirky, and the location is unique and well-developed. I hope this is just the first of many adventures for this 'Tenacious Protector' and her pals."

—Neil S. Plakcy, author c

Bingo
Barge
Murder

JESSIE CHANDLER

A Shay O'Hanlon Caper

Bingo Barge Murder

MIDNIGHT INK
WOODBURY, MINNESOTA

First Edition
First Printing, 2011

Book design and format by Donna Burch
Cover design by Lisa Novak
Cover illustration © Rick Lovell
Editing by Nicole Edman

Midnight Ink, an imprint of Llewellyn Worldwide Ltd.

Library of Congress Cataloging-in-Publication Data
Chandler, Jessie.
  Bingo barge murder : a Shay O'Hanlon caper / Jessie Chandler. — 1st ed.
      p. cm.
   ISBN 978-0-7387-2596-3
   1. Murder—Investigation—Fiction. 2. Minneapolis (Minn.)—Fiction. I. Title.
   PS3603.H3568B56 2011
   813'.6—dc22
                                  2010052307

Midnight Ink
Llewellyn Worldwide Ltd.
2143 Wooddale Drive
Woodbury, MN 55125-2989
www.midnightinkbooks.com

Printed in the United States of America

For Mom, who I hope is watching from above and laughing in delight; and for Lucky Dawg, whose tongue was legendary and whose canine heart was solid gold.
You are both loved and forever missed.

ACKNOWLEDGMENTS

This endeavor could never have come to fruition without the help and support of a number of people.

Thank you doesn't even begin to cover it, but here goes … to my awesome acquisitions editor, Terri Bischoff; my crack production editor, Nicole Edman; my amazing cover designer, Lisa Novak; publicist extraordinaire Courtney Colton; and to Midnight Ink/Llewellyn Worldwide for giving my writing this chance to shine.

For believing in me even when I lost faith, encouraging me to follow my dreams, and putting up with the hours and days I was there but really wasn't, an immense amount of gratitude and love goes out to my wife and partner, Betty. There is no way on earth I could have done this without your unflappable enthusiasm.

To JM Redmann and Micky Knight. Without the two of you, I'd have never put my fingers on a keyboard.

Thank you to Ellen Hart, who gave me the courage to believe; and Lori L. Lake, for continuing to guide me safely through writing's treacherous territory. I am happily indebted to you both.

My Hartless Murderers: Joan Murphy Pride, TJ Roth, and Brian Landon—you are my rock.

Pat & Gary at Once Upon a Crime Mystery Bookstore in Minneapolis, Ruta Skujins at True Colors Bookstore, and all my Borders peeps—I can't begin to thank you for your support and encouragement.

I want to thank NaNoWriMo, BABA's Pat Cronin, Chris Paynter, Judy Kerr, Sharon Carlson, Verda Foster, Lori L. Lake, and Mary Beth Panichi for their advice and assistance. To my friends and family: April McGuire, Angel & Monte Hight, Pearl Hedlund, Paul & Sue Hedlund, Mary Hedlund-Blomberg & Gene, Susie & Scott Augustson, Alyssa Augustson, Jean Janeksela, Alice Parsons, Marie Oslund, Bill Anding, Terry & Wendy Chandler, Jim & Gayle Knutson, Betty Jean Turner, and so many others—the unbelievable encouragement you have given has meant the world to me.

ONE

THE MORNING THAT UPENDED my usually uneventful existence was balmy for mid-November in Minneapolis. Sunlight beamed through wispy white clouds floating low in a pale blue, postcard sky. In the backyard behind my café, the Rabbit Hole, more commonly known as the Hole, I heaved a paper bag full of coffeehouse castoffs into a recycling bin that sat beneath an old maple tree. A car crept along the alley behind me, and I glanced over my shoulder to watch a Minneapolis Police Department squad car pass by.

I pivoted to head inside when someone grabbed my sweatshirt and jerked me backward, almost off my feet. Too surprised to do anything else, I stumbled and fought to keep my balance. I was dragged a few long steps through a side door into an old double-car garage. Dusty darkness shrouded my sight as if I'd been blindfolded. It all happened so fast that I didn't have a chance to utter a sound, although my pulse went from seventy to about a thousand in three seconds flat.

My shirt was released, and more in reaction than with any real plan, I whirled toward the threat. My fist actually connected solidly with some body part.

"Goddamn it, Shay!"

My arm fell to my side, and I squinted through the dust cloud our scuffle had kicked up. "Coop?"

"Jeez, I think you gave me a fat lip. Damn, you have a fast fist for a girl."

Anger overtook panic. My knuckles smarted as I shook out my hand. "What the hell? We're not seven years old anymore, you know. One of these days you're going to wind up with a whole lot more than a fat lip." I propped myself against the rusty door of my truck, using it to help support my shock-weak legs. My best and sometimes most idiotic friend, Nicholas Christopher Cooper, Coop to me, tended to attract trouble. The man is a cross between a computer genius and a drama queen.

"Shay, listen. I've got to tell—"

"For the love of—" I interrupted, my heart still rocketing. "You could have talked to me outside, you big oaf!" I glared at him. "What's wrong with, 'Shay, psst, come here, I want to talk to you.' Or how about, 'Hey Shay, step into the garage with me for a minute.' Or what about saying hello like a normal human being?"

"I'm sorry, okay? There's a cop car right outside the fricking door and…" Coop trailed off and settled his big hands on my shoulders, forcing me to face him. Grime-covered windows long ago ceased to allow more than a trickle of light inside the musty garage, but my eyes had adjusted. I took in the pinched, terrified expression on Coop's face. For once, he was even paler than me. Shaggy, tangled ash-blond hair fell into his eyes, and his chest

2

heaved as if he'd just completed a triathlon. At six-four, he towered over me by a good seven inches, a sapling-thin scarecrow.

My anger dissipated in an exhale. I'd never seen my lifelong friend in such an agitated state. Even back when we'd gotten into typical-teenager hot water, he'd never looked like he was going to stroke out or throw up on me, unless he had bonged one too many beers. "What's wrong?"

"I'm in serious trouble."

"Trouble like you knocked up the preacher's daughter, or trouble like you lost your job and can't pay your rent again?"

Coop fingered his wounded lip. "They're after me."

I stared at him for a long minute, exasperation fighting patience. "Someone's always after you. Last month it was the IRS. At Christmas you were sure the FBI was monitoring your cell. I'm shocked someone from the Looney Bin hasn't hauled your ass off to the psych ward."

"I'm serious. This is real. The police are after me."

"For what? More illegalities instigated by the Green Beans?"

Coop drew himself up to his full height. "The Green Beans for Peace and Preservation don't instigate anything. We preserve nature's way, you know that. It's not our fault the cops don't appreciate our attempts to save the planet."

"Jesus. What's going on now?"

Coop eyed me a moment longer, then looked away. He seemed to deflate the way a rubber life raft would after a nasty shark bite. His fingers pushed into his temples so hard his knuckles turned white. I watched his Adam's apple bob up and down as I waited.

He pulled a crushed pack of Marlboros from a hip pocket and lit up, sucking the fumes in deep. Finally he whispered hoarsely, "Murder."

"Murder?" I made a sound of disgust. "Whatever." Coop wouldn't hurt any living being. He felt guilty when he killed a bloodsucking mosquito.

"Hang on, I'm serious." He took another long drag from the cigarette.

Seriously paranoid, I thought, but held my tongue. "What'd you do, run over a squirrel's tail with your bike?"

He ran a visibly trembling hand through his hair. "I wish."

I waited a beat. "For Christ's sake, I'm not a mind reader here."

"Yeah, I … it's—Kinky's dead."

"Your boss is dead?"

Stanley Anderson, better known as Kinky thanks to his rather varied and public sexual appetites, was the manager of the equally sleazy Pig's Eye Bingo Barge, a gambling establishment that made its home on the banks of the Mississippi between Minneapolis and St. Paul. Coop had been working there for the past eight months, running the computer and telephone systems, the steadiest job he'd had in years.

"What happened?" I asked.

"I went down to the barge this morning about eight to talk to him. The place was crawling with cops, crime scene tape, the whole works."

"What the hell were you doing up at that time? You haven't been out of the sack before noon in years."

He shook his head in a dazed sort of way as he stubbed the cigarette out on the sole of his shoe. "Trying to save my job."

"What?"

"Kinky canned me."

"Why?"

"This past weekend, the Green Beans were at Pickering Park trying to stop the city from cutting down a bunch of trees that border the street. The city's going to widen the road and let even more cars whip by a park that's always loaded with kids." Coop's eyes were a deep shade of blue, bright even in the garage. They took on a glow as he spoke.

"How does Kinky figure into this?"

"A bunch of us were arrested Sunday, and I didn't get out of the joint until yesterday. I missed my twelve o'clock shift." Punctuality was one of Coop's biggest challenges.

"I knew Kinky was going to be pissed, but I figured he'd at least let me explain." Coop scuffed the dirty cement with the toe of his tennis shoe. "I walked into the office and he told me to hand over my keys and get out. I forgot the key ring at home, so he yelled at me to get out of his face and come back in the morning to turn them in. I get there this morning and the cops have yellow tape—"

"God, Coop, get to the point."

"Jeez, I'm trying. Kinky's dead. Someone smashed his head in with that ugly bronzed bingo marker he has in his office. You remember it?"

"Who could forget that 'legendary' thing he used when he won all that money down at the Magical Pond."

The Magical Pond was an Indian gaming casino southwest of the Twin Cities. Kinky became a quasi-celebrity after winning big bucks on Mega Stakes Bingo. Kinky bronzed the dauber, a big polish-sausage-sized bingo marker, and kept it in his office as a way to brag about his winnings. The job was botched, though, and it came out of the bronzing process almost twice its size and weight, and the entire episode turned into one of those urban legends that was actually true.

"What does that have to do with you?"

"The dauber. I picked it up off Kinky's desk last night when he was yapping at me in his office. I remember rolling it from hand to hand watching his eyes bug out as he yelled. I might have *fantasized* about taking a whack at him with it, but I didn't, I swear!"

"So what?"

"Don't you see, Shay? My fingerprints are all over it."

Oh. Now things were beginning to make sense. It was my turn to slide fingers through my now-going-every-which-way hair. The last few minutes must have added some more grays to the black strands on my scalp.

"Rocky was hanging around with the crowd gathered behind the yellow tape." Coop closed his eyes as he lost himself in memory. "He scooted right over and told me he found Kinky on the floor, dauber next to him. Blood all over. He's the one who called 911." Rocky was a mentally slow, forty-something sprite who did errands and odd jobs for Kinky. He was a character and befriended many bingo regulars and staff, Coop included.

Coop said, "They have my prints from my Green Beans arrests. They're gonna think I did it, and I don't have an alibi for last night."

"Maybe you should be up front, go and talk to the cops, explain—"

"Oh God, Shay. No way. They won't believe me. I don't want to go back to jail. You know what they do to vegetarians in jail?" He shuddered.

"So where were you last night?"

"After I talked to Kinky, I biked around. For hours. I didn't want to lose this job, you know? Eventually I went home. Late. My roommate wasn't there. Didn't come home. Must have spent the night at her boyfriend's."

Thoughts raced through my brain as I tried to process Coop's words. I knew he could handle a night in jail when it was for a good cause and he'd be sprung in a day or two, but being locked up for an extended period of time on murder charges could snuff the light out of him. Not to mention that the prison population would have a heyday with my granola-munching friend. It would destroy Coop.

My insides started the slow boil that occurred every time someone I cared about was threatened. I forced myself to breathe evenly to quell the semi-terrifying trait I'd inherited from my alcoholic father. When that roiling began, I had to really watch it. Occasionally those emotions overcame my rational side, and I could say or do things I wasn't proud of. All my life, something compelled me to root for the underdog, stand up for my friends and family—regardless of their ability to handle things themselves—and occasionally I lost the firm grip I usually had on common sense, consequences be damned. High school friends dubbed me the Tenacious Protector, TP for short. It was funny then, but now ... not so much. I felt myself begin to slip into that mode as Coop spoke.

"They're coming for me, Shay. I can feel it. Help me fix this. You always know how to make things right." Coop wrapped long arms around himself. Haggard and worn down, he suddenly appeared much older than his thirty-one years.

Before either of us could utter another word, the side door Coop dragged me through burst open with a resounding bang. Coop dove past me around the back of the truck while I stood statue still, caught like a raccoon rummaging through the garbage can.

TWO

BRIGHT SUNLIGHT STREAMED INSIDE the garage, blinding me. My eyes struggled to adjust to the abrupt glare. An indistinct form filled the doorway and a familiar voice boomed, "What the hell are you two doing shut up in this filthy place?"

The voice belonged to Edwina Quartermaine, the sixty-three-year-old-going-on-sixteen force of nature who owned the multi-story Victorian that housed the Rabbit Hole. My apartment was directly above the café, and her two-level living space took up the rear of the century-old building.

Edwina, my mother's best friend, lived next door to us when I was a kid. I'd called her Eddy instead of Mrs. Quartermaine ever since the day my mom's car was broadsided, nearly killing Eddy and me. Eddy saved my life, but my mother and Eddy's youngest boy, Neil, weren't as fortunate. I was seven years old, and my world—both our worlds—were ripped to shreds. Eddy helped piece mine back together, and she's been my life glue ever since.

Relief washed me like a monsoon, and for the second time in five minutes, my knees threatened to give out on me.

Coop crept slowly from the depths of the garage and explained his dilemma one more time.

After digesting the information, Eddy insisted we calm down with some of her infamous hot chocolate, a unique concoction of cocoa, booze, and some top-secret ingredient that tasted like a cross between anise and cinnamon. She was all about thinking things through before we made any (in her words) bonehead moves.

The late fall day had turned into a bittersweet reminder of the summer past, mixed with a chilly harbinger of things to come. We tramped across the drive to the back door of Eddy's apartment, and I hoped the crispness wasn't any kind of cosmic indication of what was destined for Coop.

Once Eddy had us settled at the worn table in her vanilla-scented kitchen, she whipped up her sure-fire remedy. The homey scene did little to calm me, though. We were going to need a whole lot of her spiked hot chocolate to fix this problem.

Short and slightly plump, Eddy had smooth, dark-brown skin, a ready smile, and salt-and-pepper hair trimmed close to her skull. She was more persistent than The Little Engine That Could. She steadfastly refused to grow old and was as spry and energetic as a woman half her age, regularly outlasting me on our almost daily jog around the neighborhood. It helped that she was always an on-the-go kind of gal who thought nothing of heading up to the Boundary Waters and camping for weeks at a time during the summer. Before she retired, her job as an inner city elementary school counselor kept her on her toes and in touch with the changing times.

A year earlier, on my thirtieth birthday, I dared Eddy to go skydiving with me. But the joke was on me when she took me up on it; I was terrified that the woman who'd practically raised me would clock-out during freefall. Not only did she not have a coronary, the crazy woman decided to do it again.

"Alrighty," Eddy said. "We need to think about this problem like they do on *Law & Order*." You could call Eddy a crime show fanatic. "Nicholas—" Eddy always used Coop's given name— "first, think about who might have wanted this Kinky dead."

Coop swirled his mug and stared as the liquid spun. "About every customer on the Bingo Barge at one time or another."

Eddy scowled. "Young man, that's not helpful. We need some solid suspects. Haven't you seen or heard Kinky—Sweet Jesus, I can't call a dead man 'Kinky.' What's this poor man's real name?" The crease between Eddy's eyes was on the verge of becoming cavernous.

"Stanley," I supplied, attempting to stop the corners of my mouth from turning up in amusement. If she could read my thoughts, Eddy would surely give me a whack for disrespecting the dead.

"Okay, who has Stanley been having words with lately?"

"He's always in someone's face about something," Coop said, "but I haven't been around the last few days to see who he pissed off lately."

We sat sipping in silence, the only sound the occasional plunk of water dripping from the kitchen faucet. A thought occurred to me, and I sat forward, leaning on my elbows. "Coop, what about

Rocky? He's always around, his ears are wide open. I bet he knows who Kinky was clashing with."

Coop brightened, his head bobbing slowly. "You might be right." Then his face fell. "But he's a night owl. And once he's on his feet, he's always with people, either at the Bingo Barge or hanging out on the block outside his boarding house. If I try to talk to him, someone'll see me and turn me in for the huge reward I'm sure the cops are already offering up on *America's Most Wanted*. I can see it now. 'Nick Cooper, wanted dead or alive.'"

"For goodness sake, stop being so morbid." Eddy shifted her gaze to me. "Shay, do you know this Rocky?"

"Yeah." Coop and I bought Rocky lunch at Popeye's on Lake Street once in awhile, and we sometimes played catch with him afterward. We always teased him that he should be pitching for the Twins with his wicked, deadly accurate fastball.

The munchkin man was an odd duck, and his mind didn't work like a regular person's. No one knew exactly what made Rocky tick the way he did. He had to be autistic or a savant of some kind. At any rate, he was high functioning and lived on his own. The man had numerous personality quirks, with communication one of the biggest. Would he talk to me without Coop around? If he didn't know someone, he'd barely speak, and if he said anything at all, he'd cough up only the very basics. If he was pushed, he locked up like a bank after hours. But once Rocky chilled and got to know you better, he wouldn't shut up. Who knew where I fell in his conversational spectrum.

Eddy poked me in the shoulder. "You're going to go look for Rocky and have a word with him."

Coop said, "You aren't going to find him till after five or six. If you find him at all."

"You hush, child." Eddy patted Coop's hand. "Shay, wait till after the supper rush when the café's settled down. If you don't have anyone coming in for the night, Kate can cover for you, or if she can't, I will."

Kate McKenzie was a good friend and my business partner. We'd gone to college together, after which we'd each tried to fit into conventional nine-to-five life and failed abysmally. Eventually we pooled our resources and, with Eddy's donation of business space, opened the café. Five years later we had a couple of employees and a fairly successful enterprise. No one was getting rich, but we weren't begging for change at the corner of Hennepin and Dunwoody either.

"We have someone scheduled for the evening shift," I said.

Eddy turned her attention back to Coop. "You need a place to hide out. I know I should tell you to turn yourself in, boy, let the wheels of justice churn you out in short order, but I know better than to believe in that nonsense. I've seen too many good people get run over by those wheels and left for dead. 'Course most of the time, things turn out fine, but sometimes it's better to take matters into your own hands."

Coop swallowed hard. Emotion was getting to him, and he struggled for composure. He cleared his throat. "Eddy, thank you for believing me."

She waved her hand. "I've helped folks deal with far worse in my lifetime. We'll get it straightened out. First things first, though. Let's get you into the loft."

I looked sharply at Eddy. "What loft?"

13

"The loft above the garage."

I raised an eyebrow. "Like I said, what loft? You said there's only an old attic full of crap in the garage." Then my other eyebrow rose to meet the first. "Oh. There's no attic full of crap."

"No attic full of crap."

Coop watched our exchange, his head moving between Eddy and me. "What on earth are you guys talking about?"

Eddy smiled mysteriously. "You never know who might need a safe place to hunker down. The attic is actually a loft that has been used for a long time by good people who needed safe refuge. People just like you."

———

Eddy bustled Coop away while Kate and I spent the next few hours making drinks and bullshitting with customers. Kainda Hannesen popped in, a professor who'd been coming to the Hole for the last few years. Kate had the hots for her in a bad way and was frustrated as hell that she couldn't put a Kainda notch on her belt. Kainda was tall with thick, almost-frizzy-it-was-so-curly black hair and skin that was perpetually golden. I myself felt a twinge of interest now and then, but I wasn't about to go toe-to-toe with Kate. And anyway, I tried to make it a policy not to see women who forked over dough to keep our establishment running. Good thing one of us felt that way, or we'd be out of business at the rate Kate went through ladies.

I cleaned what needed cleaning, and then cleaned what didn't. Time is a funny thing. Sometimes minutes and hours fly by at supersonic speed, and other times you wonder if the clocks went on strike and stopped working altogether. This was definitely an on-strike moment.

The Rabbit Hole was not sizable, but it was cozy. The café was off Hennepin Avenue on 24th Street in Uptown, not far from Sebastian Joe's Ice Cream Café, a place I frequented.

Inside the coffee shop, eight round tables with French café chairs were scattered in front of a glass counter filled with sandwiches and sweets. In two corners we'd arranged four overstuffed armchairs.

A big stone fireplace took up one wall, and the huge hearth was a popular place to hang when the temperatures fell and the nights darkened prematurely. Aromatic coffee blended with the fragrance of the I'd Tell You My Recipe But Then I'd Have To Kill You cinnamon rolls Kate regularly supplied. The walls were painted warm, swirling yellows, browns, and reds.

Lost in thought, I hunched over one of the tables and scrubbed at a particularly sticky mocha-caramel latte spill, wondering for the fifty-seventh time if not telling Kate what was going on was the right thing to do. Knowing her love of gossip and her sometimes endearing, sometimes crazy-making tendency to speak before thinking, I convinced myself that keeping my trap zipped was best for now. My clashing thoughts vanished in a blink when someone, or actually two someones, hovered directly in front of me.

A dark-skinned black man, almost as tall as Coop but with a Schwarzenegger build, stood a half step behind a woman who exuded an Outta My Way or I'll Kick Your Ass attitude. Indigo-colored jeans hugged her curves in interesting places, and a lightweight, fawn-colored leather jacket covered her navy t-shirt. A few strands of chestnut hair had worked their way loose from her rough ponytail and floated around her face. Sunglasses rested atop her head, and rich, deep-brown eyes assessed me.

My inner "who's-this-babe" meter gave a thrumming jolt until my eyes came to rest on the police shield secured in the leather wallet in her hand. I snapped my gaze back up to her face. Recognition dawned as she flipped the badge closed and pocketed it.

I slowly straightened, hoping I had enough air to speak, and shot a glance toward Kate, whose eyes were on the woman staring at me.

"Detective Bordeaux," I said. Breathe. "Been awhile."

The corner of her mouth quirked. "It has. Shay O'Hanlon, this is Detective Tyrell Johnson." She jerked a thumb at the man next to her.

I nodded. My mind bounced around like a super ball in a tin box.

Minneapolis Detective JT Bordeaux had been a regular in the Hole for many months, up until a little over a year ago, when she'd gotten transferred from Vice to Homicide. Both Kate and I had admitted to a certain fascination when she first started frequenting the café. Despite some rather enjoyable flirtation, I'd never acted on my impulses, keeping my self-imposed touch-no-customer rule well in hand.

Kate, however, with her insatiable thirst for conquering an intriguing romantic challenge, had put JT on top of her priority list. Try as she might, she hadn't gotten any further than perfecting JT's favorite drink and scoring big in the tip department. Her quest had been abruptly cut short when the detective's transfer came through and she stopped coming by for her caffeine fix.

I quickly tamped down an inappropriate primal response that hit me low in the gut, and frankly, surprised me. I guess it'd been a long time.

"We'd like to ask you a few questions about Nicholas Cooper." JT's voice was honey, her dark eyes granite.

Holy hell in a hand basket. I needed to refocus, fast.

"Questions?" I finally managed. Too many angles were floating through my mind, and my brain took the easy way out by simply shutting down.

"About what?" I asked, as my attention redirected itself to our current problem and I concentrated on putting a polite, blank look on my face. My tripping heart began a steady slam in my chest. The rag I'd been using to wipe the tables dripped as I squeezed it hard, trying to hide my trembling hands. "Has something happened to Coop?"

She said evenly, "Not that we know of. We have some questions for him. Mind if we sit down?"

Man, when she was working, she was one serious, to-the-point officer. We settled at one of the tables near the window. Kate floated over to us, pixie-like. She glanced at Johnson and then settled her twin lasers on JT. If looks could set the hook, the detective would have been reeled right into Kate's waiting net.

"Anything I can get you all?" Her words encompassed the table but her gaze remained glued on Detective Bordeaux. Table service wasn't Hole protocol, but when a hot babe showed up, Kate was willing to go the extra mile. "Aren't you a sight for sore eyes," she told the detective. "Can I get you your usual?"

I glanced at Detective Johnson, who was busy trying to suppress a smile, and I squinted at Kate, willing her to back off. She ignored me and shot her signature You Are So Back In My Sights gaze at JT, who ordered her usual cappuccino with double espresso while Johnson declined a beverage. Kate gave me a toothy grin and scooted off to make JT her drink.

Perched warily in my chair, I said to JT, "Still a caffeine junkie, huh?"

Silence ensued, and my ears burned in mild embarrassment. I wondered if it was detective modus operandi to ignore the unrequested comments of the interrogated. Detective Johnson bailed me out. He eyed my t-shirt, asking if I'd seen the last Minnesota Wild hockey game. Johnson chatted while I uh-huhed and um-hmmed about the possibilities of the Wild's chance at playoff action for the upcoming season.

Kate returned with a steaming beverage and handed it to JT, who took a sip. She gave Kate a quick nod of satisfaction, and set the glass mug on the table.

"You haven't lost your touch, I see," JT said to Kate.

"No, I haven't lost any touch at all." Kate eyed her provocatively. "Let me know if you need anything else."

JT turned to me as Kate sashayed away. "So, Shay, how long have you known Mr. Cooper?"

I tried to remember if she'd ever run into Coop when she'd stopped by the café, but I couldn't. It was so odd to hear him referred to as Mr. Cooper. "We grew up in the same neighborhood, went to the same schools, and remained friends through adolescent hell."

Detective Johnson rested his arms on the table, his heavily muscled shoulders bulging under his shirt. "Ms. O'Hanlon, when was the last time you saw Nicholas Cooper?"

Cut straight to the chase, why don't you? I wondered what the penalty was for lying through my teeth to the cops. However, my Tenacious Protector side had started bouncing around like Tigger on steroids.

"I think the last time I saw Coop was this past Friday. He was getting ready to head over to Pickering Park with his environmental group." Thank God he mentioned that in the garage. "They were going to protest the removal of some trees." That much was true. "Is that what this is about?"

The two detectives glanced at each other and then leveled their stares back at me. JT said, her voice silky now, "So you haven't seen Mr. Cooper all weekend?"

I shook my head as I thought about Coop in the garage not a hundred yards away. I was going straight to hell. No passing GO, no collecting two hundred dollars, and there would be no Get Out of Jail Free cards.

"Is he in trouble?" I stared directly into JT's eyes. The hard demeanor she presented when she'd first spoken softened, but her features remained impassive. "We're not sure. An incident occurred at his workplace and we just want to talk to him."

"What kind of incident?" I said the words as nonchalantly as I could, but my hands were curled tight around the base of my chair to keep them still.

Detective Johnson's voice rumbled. "Mr. Cooper's employer was murdered last night."

"What?" My eyebrows shot up of their own accord, even though this wasn't news. "You're kidding. What happened?"

Could they tell I was spewing tall tales? Were they about to whip out the cuffs?

Instead of flashing metal, Detective Johnson said, "We've got some video showing multiple persons entering and exiting the office where the murder took place. Your friend was seen on the tape leaving in a rather agitated state."

Videotape. Could it clear Coop? If it did, why were the cops looking for him? Speaking carefully, I said, "You think Coop killed Kinky? He won't kill a mosquito. Seriously."

Johnson hitched an eyebrow. "You know Stanley Anderson?"

Whoa. Open mouth, insert grimy shoe. "I met him a few times when I've gone to see Coop at work. And Coop wouldn't lay a finger on his boss." I didn't add that Coop was so grossed out by Kinky that you couldn't pay him to put a pinkie on the man.

JT eyed me for a beat. "We don't know who killed Mr. Anderson." Then her dark eyes softened again for a moment. "You're sure you haven't seen Mr. Cooper today, Shay?" Those eyes intrigued me, even as I watched them shift back into assessment mode.

"No, I haven't." The lie came a bit easier this time. I wanted to ask them if they had fingerprints off the dauber, but they hadn't yet told me what the murder weapon was. Man, it was as hard to withhold information as it was to lie. If the cops didn't have fingerprints, maybe they were just running down all of the people on the video and asking questions. How long did it take to identify fingerprints? Hours? Days?

They peered at me silently. I decided some interrogation of my own couldn't make matters much worse. Maybe they'd tell me something that we could use to help Coop. "How did Kinky die?"

Johnson shook his head. "I'm afraid that's not something we can discuss."

Detective Bordeaux dug into her jeans pocket and threw a five on the table. "If you can think of anything that might help us, or if you see Mr. Cooper, please give me a call. Actually, better yet, have him call me." She handed me her card, eyes still glued to me like a hungry animal patiently waiting for feeding time. I wanted to squirm, figuratively and literally, under that hot gaze. Did she just want information from me?

After thanking me for my less-than-helpful help, the detectives threaded their way through the room to the front door. Before Detective Bordeaux stepped outside, she called out, "Kate, that capp was just like it used to be. Thanks."

Kate saluted JT, and I grinned weakly. After the door shut amid the chime of bells, I collapsed into the chair with my head in my arms. My mind was a blur of dread and guilt, mixed with some intriguing thoughts about some rather unethical but very hot ways Detective Bordeaux could try to pry the truth out of me. I had no idea if my untimely re-attraction was one-sided, but under different circumstances, I could easily have been persuaded to find out. Unless, of course, Kate beat me to it.

THREE

For a half hour, I dodged the questions Kate kept lobbing about my visit with the Daring Duo. I was relieved when my longtime pal Doyle Malloy stopped in late in the afternoon for coffee and a chat. He was my first, last, and only boyfriend. Convinced he'd turned me into a lesbian, he often laughed about our doomed relationship. He was a Minneapolis detective who only worked high-level homicides. Maybe I could get something out of him to help Coop.

Once he settled at a table, I sat across from him. "So Doyle, you hear about the murder on the Pig's Eye Bingo Barge?"

"Yeah, I heard about—ah damn!" Doyle swore as the sip of coffee meant for his mouth was sucked up by the front of his white oxford shirt. He swiped halfheartedly at the tan-colored stain.

I stifled a laugh. "Don't worry. It matches that mustardy-looking smear there by your pocket."

"I don't know why I try." He sighed. "I heard Bordeaux and Johnson are on that one. By the way, Bordeaux's still footloose and fancy-free, on the market." He raised an eyebrow at me.

Doyle knew I'd been fascinated from afar by JT when she used to stop in, and for some reason he felt it was his lifelong duty to try to hook me up with someone. In all actuality, he sucked as a matchmaker.

I pointedly ignored his addendum. "Any suspects?" I asked.

"I'm just sayin'." He held his hands up in appeasement as he narrowed an eye at me. "Anyway, I know they're working a couple leads, looking for one of the staff members." Doyle scratched at the stubble on his cheek. "I don't think I heard who …" He trailed off and looked at me. "Doesn't Nick Cooper work on that tub?"

Doyle wasn't what I'd consider friends with Coop, but we'd all gone to school together, and he knew Coop and I were close. "Yeah," I said, "he does." Or did, at any rate.

Then Doyle moved conspiratorially toward me, and I almost leaned away from him, afraid of what he was going to say next. He whispered, "Rumor has it the guy was whacked by an unhappy husband, know what I mean?"

Well, that was better than a rumor that an unhappy ex-employee named Nicholas Cooper beaned Kinky on the melon for firing him.

Doyle finished his coffee and took off. I took the espresso machine apart and put it back together for entertainment until our evening relief arrived.

Kate left with a wave and a promise to pry the big secret out of me in the morning. I exited stage right to hunt down Eddy and Coop, who were at Eddy's kitchen table knee-deep into supper.

While they downed leftovers, I chewed on some antacids I found in one of Eddy's kitchen drawers. My stomach was usually unflappable, but having *Coop* and *murder* in the same sentence did a number on my gastric fortitude. I briefed the two of them on my exploits with Minneapolis' finest and Kate the Inquisitor until it was time for me to go find Rocky.

At seven o'clock, I loaded myself into my pickup. After circling Rocky's block four times, I spotted the familiar puffy green jacket he lived in year-round. A ratty, wool-lined aviator hat sat cockeyed on his head. He leaned against the side of an abandoned building in the semi-darkness, his mouth moving a mile a minute, chatting with the air around him, or maybe with ghostly spirits I couldn't see. You never know. Relief buzzed through me, almost like having one too many beers. I pulled to the curb and rolled down the passenger window.

"Hey, Rocky," I yelled.

Rocky's eyes focused on my vehicle, but he didn't recognize it, or me. His lips stopped moving, and he froze.

"Rocky, it's me, Shay," I said, praying he wouldn't take off.

He squinted. Then a grin spread slowly across his wide face, exposing crooked teeth. He rushed over to the open window.

"Shay O'Hanlon." His entire body vibrated happiness in seeing a familiar face. "You drive a pretty blue Toyota Tundra, Shay O'Hanlon." He ran his fingers over the smooth paint.

"Thank you, Rocky. Are you hungry?"

Rocky's grin grew. "Always hungry."

"Hop in. Popeye's?"

"Popeye's. My favorite." He opened the door and clambered in. "Always wear your seatbelt," he mumbled, tugging the strap across his round body and clicking it home.

The restaurant was on Lake Street, a busy thoroughfare running through Uptown and the lakes area. We pulled into the parking lot and tramped inside. Rocky ordered spicy fried chicken with rice and beans. Food still wasn't something my insides were much interested in. I procured myself a Coke and we found a table and sat down.

Rocky said in a very serious voice, "I want to thank you for this most delicious meal, Shay O'Hanlon."

"You're welcome, Rocky."

As he burrowed his way through the beans, I asked, "Did you see Coop this morning?"

Rocky looked at me, his oddly beautiful golden eyes big, his mouth full. "Yes, yes I did see Nick Coop, Shay O'Hanlon." His attention returned to the plate and he shoveled another scoopful in.

Coop had given me some "talking to Rocky" advice. If he felt safe with me, I could ask him questions and he'd do his best to answer. Conversely, if he felt threatened, he'd answer with a single word. If I was lucky.

And where was my luck going to land me? I sipped from my straw and swallowed, considering my next words. "What did you tell Coop about Stanley Anderson?"

His eyes flicked up to me and then to his plate. "I told Nick Coop that Mr. Stanley was lying on the floor in his office. That big bingo marker Mr. Stanley liked so much was on the floor by his head. Gross." The fork sped to Rocky's mouth again.

"Do you know what happened to Mr. Stanley, Rocky?" I asked, adopting his name for the dead man.

"You must chew every bite twenty-six times, Shay O'Hanlon."

Wow. "Uh huh. What happened to Mr. Stanley?"

The chewing didn't slow, but some food particles came flying out as he spoke. "Someone bonked him on the noodle and killed him."

"Do you know who bonked him?"

"Must remember to drink when you eat," he announced, and took a few healthy slugs of his pop, his throat working as the liquid slid down. Then he said, "Nick Coop didn't hurt Mr. Stanley."

"I know he didn't," I said softly. "Did someone say he did?"

Jaw muscles bunched as Rocky chowed down. "The police people asked me about him."

I closed my eyes and inhaled, willing my heart not to leap out of my chest. I blinked, then said, "You know he didn't have anything to do with that, right?"

Rocky hunched over his plate and shoveled another forkload in. "No way did Nick Coop hurt Mr. Stanley. Nick Coop could never ever hurt anything."

"Rocky," I said very softly. "Look at me."

He slowly slid his gaze to mine. I said, "I know Coop didn't hurt Mr. Stanley. But do you have any idea who might have done this bad thing to Mr. Stanley?"

Rocky's cheek twitched. "Lots of people were mad at Mr. Stanley, Shay O'Hanlon." The beans finished, his attention moved on to the rice. He ate one thing at a time, making sure not to mix the different foods on his plate.

I sighed. This was worse than talking to a toddler. "Who was mad at Mr. Stanley?"

Without moving his head he said, "coopmsritabuzzrileyms—," and trailed off into unintelligible garble as he finished his twenty-sixth chew and swallowed.

"What?"

He repeated his words without taking a breath.

Coop's name was at the beginning, and a couple of the other names sounded vaguely familiar. Coop had lots of crazy tales about the Bingo Barge regulars, and I figured Rocky's list had to encompass a few of those bingo nuts.

I pulled a pen out of my pocket and wrote *Coop* on a napkin. I showed it to Rocky, and he nodded enthusiastically.

"Will you tell me the names one more time?" My pen hovered over the napkin.

He gave me a disgusted look but begrudgingly said, "coopms-ritabuzzrileymslavonneandsomebig—," ending in more gibberish. Then he said very clearly, "Buzz Riley's a very bad man, Shay O'Hanlon."

I hid a grin and quickly scrawled *Rita*, *Buzz Riley*, and *Lavonne* while Rocky slurped the last of the contents in his cup. Coop had told me some run-ins he'd had with Mr. Riley, and he indeed sounded like a first-class ass. What did "some big" mean? A big man? A big woman? A big bingo ball? "Hey, Rocky, what did you mean when you say 'and some big'?"

"I am full now, Shay O'Hanlon. Thank you."

It seemed my Q&A session had come to a close.

Rocky chattered as I drove him home. The names he gave me ran over and over through my head. At his boarding house, he opened the door to get out of the truck, turned to me, and reached for my hand. "Shay O'Hanlon, you are not going to let anything bad happen to my friend Nick Coop." His beseeching golden eyes just about broke my heart.

"I'm going to try very hard to make sure nothing bad happens to Coop."

"Thank you, Shay O'Hanlon. Thank you." He pumped my hand, and was about to slam the door when he turned back to me. "Be sure to rotate your tires every six thousand miles, Shay O'Hanlon." Rocky gently shut the door and disappeared into his building, leaving me to repeat "coopmsritabuzzrileymslavonneandsomebig" like a mantra all the way home.

————

I trudged along the rough stone sidewalk to Eddy's back door and let myself in. I felt drained from the strange emotions of the day. After rousing Eddy from her *CSI*-induced stupor in front of the TV, she led me out to the garage. Once inside the dim garage, she flipped a switch to illuminate it with a single bare bulb.

"So how do you get up there?" I asked Eddy.

"The ladder, child." Eddy pointed to an old ladder resting against the garage wall. The wooden deathtrap was decorated with varying hues of smeared and dripped paint—remnants of Eddy's attempts at replicating interior decorating projects she had seen on the DIY network. I had been on that sorry excuse for a ladder helping with a couple of those so-called projects. I'd sworn never to step foot on the rickety contraption again.

Eddy laughed at my terror-stricken expression. "I'm pullin' your funny bone. You push that there button under the ledge." She pointed at a shelf of crusty oil cans. I stuck my hand beneath the blackened, grimy plank, and at one corner, felt the nub of a button. I bent over and peered under the shelf. Sure enough, an old-fashioned doorbell was installed on the bottom.

Eddy said, "Push it."

I pushed. A square of light appeared above us, and one of those retractable, rescue-type ladders slid down to within a couple feet of the garage floor. The opening in the ceiling glowed like a window to the heavens.

Coop's head popped upside-down through the opening.

"Hey you two," he said, then disappeared.

Eddy eyed at me. "What are you waiting for? Come on." She strode over and clambered up the ladder. She never ceased to do way more than I ever could expect. I shut my mouth, which was hanging open, and climbed up behind her.

As my head came through the trap door, I whispered, "Holy. Shit." Below me lay a musty, filthy double-car garage. The space above was completely different.

A couple of ancient lamps chased most of the shadows away. The room was only about ten feet by twelve with a pitched roof. Rough planks were laid for flooring, and were partially covered with a remnant of outdated orange shag. A neatly made up but ancient twin bed perched in a corner, along with a crib that looked as though it had seen more than its share of tantrums.

For a moment, I wondered if I'd crawled into Doc Brown's De-Lorean and traveled back to the Seventies. A little kitchen setup in one corner had a mini two-burner electric stove, a single basin sink with separate faucets for hot and cold, and a dorm-type refrigerator that was almost futuristic compared to the rest of the kitchen appliances. A modern twelve-inch TV on a two-tier cart sat above a VCR/DVD combo unit. A small camping-style toilet was stashed back under the sloped rafters. From the looks of it, stowaways must only use the emergency john when it was impossible to sneak into Eddy's apartment.

The entrance from the garage floor was situated near the mini-kitchen. After I hauled myself through the opening, Coop pulled up the ladder and pushed a button that closed the trap door by activating a jerry-rigged electrical pulley. I eyed the contraption, wondering if we could escape if the electricity died or a fire broke out.

Eddy slid into a chair at a battered card table and Coop sat next to her. "Watch your head, child," Eddy warned as I started toward the table and nearly knocked myself for a loop on a rafter in the sloped roof.

"What on earth is this … this room, doing here?" I was still having a hard time believing I was above the garage.

Eddy patted my hand. "It was built a long time ago. It's my own private Underground Railroad, a safe place for those in need. It's been used mostly by women and their children running from abusive boyfriends, husbands, that kind of thing. The Mad Knitters helped restore it a few years back." Eddy gazed around the room and sighed. "Maybe it was more than a few years. We fixed it up so it'd be almost soundproof from below, lightproof, too. It's got an electric heater, and somewhat decent ventilation, although it can get pretty close up here during the summer."

The Mad Knitters met on a semi-weekly basis at the Rabbit Hole, supposedly to make progress on their knitting skills, but they usually ended up around Eddy's kitchen table playing pinochle or poker instead. The previous summer, Eddy bestowed honorary membership upon Coop. He gamely tried but still struggled with coordinating the knitting needles and not poking his eye out. He told me more than once that he heaved a big sigh of relief when they set down the yarn and picked up the cards.

"I guess you could call all of us modern-day Harriet Tubmans. We protect anyone who fears for their safety for whatever reason." Eddy sighed again. "Too many reasons to be fearful nowadays."

I was dying to hear more about this secret room and the people who had passed through it, but I suppressed my urge to badger. Later, when we had time, Eddy had some explaining to do.

Coop eagerly leaned toward me. "What'd you find out from Rocky?"

I launched into the story, ending with the names Rocky had given me. "Msritabuzzrileymslavonneandsomebig."

Coop burst out laughing. "Nice."

"So who are they?" Eddy asked.

"He means Rita Lazar, Buzz Riley, and Lavonne Smith." Coop said. "They're all bingo players. I don't know who he means with 'and some big' though. A big huge man? We have a few that would fit that description."

I said, "Any of the people Rocky listed a possible deadly dauber wielder?"

Coop thought about that for a moment. "Rita? Man, I just can't see it, but she does have a temper from hell. Buzz Riley is just an asshole. I can see him taking a whack. Lavonne ... well, she's just plain crazy. I don't think she's lethal, though."

"Is there any chance we can get an eyeful of these bingo players?" Eddy suggested. "Maybe they're on that video the detectives told Shay about."

"I don't know," Coop said. "The system's digital. If they left the hard drive, we'd probably be able to see the video."

I asked. "Wouldn't we be able to see the video of who killed Kinky, then?"

Coop met my eyes. "If Kinky was killed after the bingo session was over, it wouldn't show. The system stops recording when the safe is locked for the night. Unless—the safe hadn't been locked yet." Coop sat up straighter. "Hey, maybe there's a chance the killer *is* on it."

Eddy shook her head. "Uh uh. If they had the killer on tape, there'd be an APB out on him and all the questioning those two detectives did would have been time wasted. They'd have come right out and said they were looking for Nicholas Cooper, Bingo Boss Brutalizer. If you watched more *Law & Order*, you'd know that."

We sat in silence for a couple of moments. I pondered how much faith we could place in the accuracy of primetime cop shows. Then I said, "I think we need to check out Kinky's office, look in his files. Maybe we can find out who he wasn't getting along with."

"Child, I do like the way you think. We can find us some rigged bingo cards or something!" Eddy's grin held lots of wattage.

"Hey, listen, you two burglar wannabes," Coop said, a frown slicing his forehead. "Bad idea. Don't you think the cops are still all over the barge?"

Eddy snorted. "You got a lot to learn about the police, Nicholas. They been there and did their crime scene stuff, and they're long gone." She rubbed her hands together like a kid about to dive into a birthday cake. "When are we gonna do the job?"

No way in hell was I traipsing out on a barge on the Mississippi River tonight. I said, "With Coop hiding out up here, time's not as critical as it would be if he were wandering the streets. Tomorrow night. I don't think it would be wise to go skipping in there during the daylight."

Coop said, "How are we going to get in? Don't you think the cops will have it locked up?"

Eddy rolled her eyes. "Boy, where is your head? Why did you go back to that barge this morning?"

Coop shrugged. "I went to talk to Kinky again and try to convince him to give me one more chance."

"And?" Eddy stared at Coop expectantly.

Comprehension flooded Coop's narrow face, and his cheeks flushed. "To give him back the keys."

Eddy sat back in her chair and crossed her arms. "Bingo."

I shook my head. "Coop, I love you, but sometimes you're a big dope."

FOUR

I ROLLED OUT OF bed after drifting in and out of sleep most of the night, a familiar honey-laden voice haunting my dreams, teasing me, taunting me to tell the truth. Awake and out of bed, I imagined that voice whispering things that weren't related to interrogating, arresting, and booking me. I tried to shake off the lingering thoughts of a certain Minneapolis detective as I automatically pulled the covers up and fluffed the pillows—thanks to years of listening to Eddy harp, "Child, you need start the day out on the right foot, and the best way to do that is to make your bed like a civilized person."

After a quick shower, I stuffed myself into a worn-at-the-knee pair of Levi's and a Rabbit Hole t-shirt. I shook out a sweatshirt and tugged it over my head as I walked out of my bedroom.

I fancied my interior décor spartan, but Eddy called it just plain cheap. A seldom-used TV and a ratty couch took up most of the living room. My other furniture consisted of my mother's antique roll-top desk and an old wooden, swivel-type office chair. I settled into the chair, its familiar creaking as comforting as it was irritating. I picked up a bill from our advertising guru Amy Connolly and whipped out a check. Amy was one person I didn't mind coughing up the dough for. When we'd hooked up with her a couple years ago, our customer count went through the roof, and our return business remained rock solid.

Done with that task, I briefly allowed myself to fall into the memory of my mom working at this very desk, trying to pay bills with money we didn't have while I happily Crayola'd secondhand coloring books on the floor next to her, never for a moment feeling like we didn't have enough. The strength of her love hadn't faded with time and could still wind around me like a warm blanket. With a deep sigh, I funneled those bittersweet thoughts neatly back into the recesses from which they'd drifted and trotted downstairs, past Eddy's French doors, through a short hall, and into the Rabbit Hole.

A few customers quietly conversed at the tables, and Jim Brickman's piano playing gently swirled from speakers mounted to the walls. Sinking into one of the cushioned chairs in the corner, I closed my eyes and rubbed my face, trying hard to convince myself that yesterday's events had been a strangely lucid and horribly vivid nightmare.

Kate stood behind the counter, her spiked fuchsia hair bobbing behind the espresso machine as she finished off a drink. She caught my eye, smiled, and moments later appeared by my side with a newspaper and a steaming hazelnut latte.

"What would I do without you?" I gratefully took the mug from her.

She perched on the padded arm of my chair. "Go out of business."

Kate was right. The woman was a human hummingbird, a front-of-house queen. When she needed to, she could move so fast you hardly realized she was doing anything at all. What she did was everything. I'd never be able to keep the place afloat without Kate. And she felt the same way about me. I was the behind-the-scenes muscle, coordinating PR, finances, orders, and whatever other pesky details came up. Neither of us could do the other's job, but together we were a great business team. It was one of the many reasons Kate and I'd never hooked up—hanky panky between business partners was the kiss of death.

"So, you mind if I borrow your cabin weekend after next? I have a," Kate paused with a smirk, "*mucho caliente muchacha* I'd like to entertain in the deep woods."

My family owned a cabin on Finch Lake outside of North Branch on forty acres of forested land. My dad hunted there in the fall, and we used the cabin year-round.

I grinned. "Be my guest. Just wash the sheets before you leave."

"Excellent. Changing the subject, are you going to tell me what was with the cops yesterday?"

I leaned my head against the cushion and groaned. "I wasn't dreaming then." So much for my vivid nightmare theory.

Kate laughed. "Unless I'm having the same dream, nope. But you know, JT's still a hot little she-devil. Wouldn't mind having a dream or two about her."

I agreed, but kept that to myself. "Believe me when I say you don't want to know."

"Ohhhh-kay, whatever. What are you going to do with your day off?" Kate asked as she stood up. She glanced at the front door, the sound of the bells attached to it chiming merrily as it opened. Kate said quietly, "Speak of the she-devil."

Sure enough, the she-devil was closing our front door. Crap. My heart thumped, and I was caught in a vortex of being strangely pleased and outright terrified. Ugh. I was not awake enough to do the question-and-answer dance.

Kate abandoned me and made a beeline back to the counter. I took a gulp of my latte, silently swearing when the hot liquid singed my tongue.

Detective Bordeaux strolled up to the counter and chatted with Kate for a moment. She hadn't yet seen me, which gave me a chance to size her up. She was a bit taller than Kate's five-six, with a solid, medium build compared to Kate's willowy body. Her dark hair was up in a ponytail again. Wearing a black blazer, faded blue jeans, and black boots with deep treads, she looked good. And more than ready to kick some bad-guy booty.

Kate bustled around making a drink for the good detective. I knew it would again be a cappuccino with a double shot. She was the type to stick with the same thing once she found something she liked. Was that how she stepped into relationships, or was she more Kate-esque, footloose and lovin' free? As JT spoke, the light from the window caught her cheek, throwing the hollows of her face into shadow. Attractive. Very attractive. She appeared the quiet, studious type, and I wondered if she liked to read. If she did, she probably went for something non-fiction and stuffy, like those big books about Important Social Issues whose authors made it onto C-SPAN's Book TV.

other than my best friend. I mentally slapped myself. Jesus, O'Hanlon. What was wrong with me?

"This capp really is excellent. I'll be in touch." With that she stood and walked to the condiment bar, grabbed a lid, and snapped it on her cup. Over her shoulder she said to me, "If you hear anything from Mr. Cooper, call me." It's wasn't a request. I swallowed hard as she said goodbye to Kate and left.

The jingle of the bells faded, and Kate returned to me, a wide grin on her face.

"You snitch," I said.

Kate raised an eyebrow, smirked. "She was nice. Tipped me five bucks."

"Taking bribes now, are you?"

"Bills, babes ... you know how it goes." Kate winked at me and floated toward a customer waiting impatiently at the counter.

———

Coop, Eddy, and I spent the balance of the afternoon and early evening planning our bingo hall break-in. Eddy, trumping our protests, refused to be left out. She assured us she'd worn clean underwear in case we were busted.

The darkness of midnight weighed heavily as we piled into Eddy's old yellow pickup and rumbled toward the Pig's Eye Bingo Barge.

"My eyes aren't as good as they used to be in the dark," Eddy said, squinting out the windshield as we zoomed down Interstate 94. I learned long ago to say multiple prayers to multiple gods whenever I climbed into a vehicle Eddy was piloting. The woman handled the pickup as if she were in a qualifying heat for a NASCAR race. Anytime we arrived at our destination in one piece, I resisted the overwhelming urge to fling myself to the ground and kiss the earth in thanks.

The stars and the moon were blotted out by clouds, and the blackness was thick behind the tall mercury vapor lights lining the freeway. It would be a good night for some B&E, provided we made it there intact.

A few minutes and a few white knuckle moments later, we pulled into a ten-car parking lot across from the street that wound along the river, about a quarter-mile from the Bingo Barge. Eddy cut the motor and switched off the headlights. Blackness engulfed us. We sat unmoving, holding our breaths, waiting to see if a squad car was going to come roaring up with lights blazing.

We'd all dressed in black, with the exception of Eddy's neon-green high tops. No amount of cajoling convinced her to put on less attention-grabbing footwear. She told us in no uncertain terms they were her lucky shoes, and she couldn't be part of a break-in without them. For our protection, Eddy also had her "Whacker," a 12-inch baseball bat she'd gotten at some long ago Twins game. Eddy hung around the Rabbit Hole often and fancied herself the unofficial Hole bouncer. She'd whip out the Whacker when she thought someone might be getting out of hand after ingesting too much caffeine. To date, she'd only clobbered one guy, and he deserved it because he'd tried to filch a handful of bills out of the till when Kate's back was momentarily turned.

Coop had the keys to the barge clenched in his fist. A portable tool kit in my pocket poked into my thigh. We each had a flashlight and a set of plastic serving gloves I'd lifted from the Hole.

I nudged Coop, who sat next to the door. "Come on. Let's get this over with." My heart thudded in my ears. I hoped Eddy's ticker was doing okay. I shook off the thought. Why was I so fixated on the state of Eddy's heart? Must be afraid she'd exit stage right before I was ready to let her go. As if I'd ever be ready.

We three huddled at the back of the truck.

"Let's walk along the side of the bank next to the river," I whispered. "We'll be less visible from the road."

"The Whacker's ready for some action. Let's go." Eddy waved her mini bat in the air, and Coop reached out and grabbed it before it thumped him in the chest.

"Keep your voices down," Coop whispered harshly. "Sounds carry over the water, you know. God, I need a smoke."

We crossed the road single file. A rolling hill ran parallel to the road, and we climbed upward, legs burning, lungs rasping. On the far side of the mound, a gentle slope led downward to a sudden ten-foot drop to the cold, dark Mississippi. I caught a whiff of eau d'fish and other odors I couldn't quite (and probably didn't want to) put my finger on.

We scurried rapidly along the river toward the blacked-out barge. The behemoth looked like a cheap, one-story rendition of the floating river casinos found in states farther south.

The barge had been painted white with dark-blue trim when first installed off of Moffat's Point, between Minneapolis and St. Paul. However, time and the harsh conditions of floating on the river had weathered the once-proud exterior. Paint peeled off the sides, looking like bark falling off a dead tree. Rust stains made the vessel appear as if it were silently crying. Even the gaudy, neon PIG'S EYE BINGO sign was unlit. It was eerie as hell.

"Why aren't there any lights on?" I asked Coop, my voice low.

"Kinky is—I mean Kinky *was* too cheap to keep them on when there's no bingo in session."

We hunkered out of sight in long, weedy grass next to the wide gangway that led to the front doors of the barge. I almost jumped out of my shoes when the floating palace of sin shifted noisily against its moorings.

The entry still had yellow police tape stretched across it. Earlier we'd discussed the pros and cons of going in through the front doors and decided that it would be safer to enter through the delivery entrance on the far end of the barge.

Eddy poked Coop in the back with her Whacker. "What are you waiting for?"

"I'm going already. Jeez." Coop hopped up and darted over the gangway and onto the deck. He hunched over and waddled like a mallard along the railing to the delivery door. Once he unlocked the door and disarmed the alarm, he waved us in.

I followed Eddy as she scooted along ahead of me, her shoes radiating green with each step. I held my breath, waiting for a bullhorn to sound, "You with the glow-in-the-dark shoes, stop right there!" But, thankfully, we all made it safely inside. The door clicked shut and we were plunged into a thick, suffocating black so pure that if there were a color for death, this would be it.

No one said a word. We strained to listen for sounds that our escapade was about to come to an arresting end until Eddy clicked on her flashlight and waved it around. We were in a windowless supply room. Coop and I flicked on our own flashlights, and Coop said in a stage whisper, "This door opens to the main hall. Kinky's office is down the gangway on the far side of the hall. We'll have to

43

shut the flashlights off when we cross the main area because of the windows, but his office doesn't have windows. We can turn the lights on without anyone seeing anything."

"Don't forget the gloves," I said. Crinkling sounds filled the room as we struggled to stuff our hands into the clear plastic serving gloves.

We were plunged into creepy blackness as we flipped the flashlights off. Coop eased the door to the bingo floor open. The odor of stale cigarette smoke and the lingering smell of greasy, fried food made my nose wrinkle.

Coop moved silently ahead of us, and we hurried to catch up to his dark form. The bingo hall was unrecognizable in the dark. By the time I thought I'd gotten a handle on where we were in the cavernous room, Coop was zinging down a hallway that housed the restrooms and Kinky's office.

Coop stopped short in front of an open door. I bounced into him and Eddy ran into me with a grunt. He whispered, "This is it."

Eddy, hanging on to me as she regained her balance, whispered, "What's the holdup? Go on in, boy."

Coop suddenly backpedaled into me. "Oh hell. No way. I got us here. Someone else can go in there first. Blood and guts… uh-uh." His voice was hoarse.

Eddy elbowed her way past us. "Outta my way, then. Swear I gotta do all the work for you kids these days." She turned on her flashlight and charged through the door. Coop and I followed in her wake.

"See, nothin' here except a big hole where the carpet's been chopped out." Eddy's flashlight stopped on a missing rectangular section of filthy gray carpet. I thought the stale air held the faintest tang of copper, but it was probably in my head.

"I think I'm gonna pass out," Coop said.

I grabbed his arm and shook him. "No, you're not. Don't you dare pass out, Nicholas Cooper." The shock of hearing his given name come out of my mouth was enough to bring him to his senses.

The light switch was next to the door. I flipped it on. We blinked in unison at the harsh fluorescent glare. A tan metal desk covered by a flat calendar sat to one side. Stains I really, really hoped were from food decorated various portions of the calendar, along with doodles and random notes jotted on the border and under some of the dates. A tired-looking computer sat beside the calendar.

A precarious mountain of papers and magazines on one corner of the desk threatened to go into a landslide at any moment. I wondered if the cops had anything to do with the mess or if it was a reflection of Kinky's organizational abilities.

A two-shelf hutch was pushed up against a wall and loaded with file folders, used or defective bingo daubers in various neon shades, and a clear plastic jar of bingo balls that looked suspiciously like glorified Ping-Pong balls. A rack stood next to it holding a computer monitor, keyboard, three hard drives, and a VCR.

A grimy loveseat and two chairs took up an entire wall, and two framed, poster-sized prints hung on the opposite wall. One of the prints portrayed abstract female body parts in various stages of undress, and the other was a portrait of a life-sized, slicked-up Kinky holding out his bronzed bingo dauber for the world to see.

More magazines were piled on the floor behind Kinky's desk, and I suppressed a shudder when I caught a glimpse of the top one. It's certainly a free world, but the content was more than I ever wanted to know about Kinky's sexual appetites. The glossy was entitled *Whips and Chains*, and a picture of a balding man graced the cover. On all fours, he wore a dog collar and nothing else. Behind him, holding a leash attached to the collar, a rubber-suited dominatrix with an evil grin cracked a wicked-looking whip.

Eddy stuck the Whacker under her arm and settled into the office chair. "The desk is mine."

"I'll go through the security hard drive." Coop made for the rack of electronics and fired up the system.

The hutch was as good a place as any for me to start. I stepped to it and poked through the piles of paper. Not much to see except letters from the Gambling Control Commission of Minnesota, bingo paperwork, and notes from workers requesting time off.

It wasn't five minutes before Coop said, "The digital files are gone. I thought they archived, but nothing's here." So much for easy answers.

Eddy was busy sifting through the sheaves of paper on the top of the desk. I pulled open the right-hand desk drawer and found it filled with pens, paperclips, a half-eaten Baby Ruth, a set of keys, and a few business cards. One card was a reminder for an appointment at DeeDee's House of Massage. Two of the business cards were from bingo equipment distributors, and another was from Schiek's, a strip joint in downtown Minneapolis.

The cops must not have deemed the business cards worthy evidence since they were still in the drawer. If I were them, I'd check into DeeDee's and see what kinds of massages were being given. I tucked the cards back in the drawer and slid it shut.

"Sweet Jesus! I'll be," Eddy said. She had an official form with the picture of a bingo player attached to it with a paper clip. The top of the paper read RELEASE and the form gave the Pig's Eye Bingo Barge permission to use the winner's image for publicity. I'd periodically seen ads in the local newspaper that showcased the big winners each week. According to Coop, the players loved it.

"That damn Margaret," Eddy said. "She skipped out on the last few Knitters meetings, told us her arthritis was acting up. Here she's been playing bingo." She squinted at the page. "Says here she won two grand." Eddy shot Coop an accusatory glare. "You knew about this all along, didn't you, you twerp?"

Coop had the sense to appear sheepish and raised his bony shoulders until they were up around his ears. "Yeah. Margaret swore me to secrecy. Sorry, Eddy."

Eddy studied the picture again, holding it close to her face. "This photo serves her right. All those wrinkles." She tossed the packet on the top of the pile. "Guess now she can pay me the poker bucks I loaned her last month."

A grin tugged at the corner of my mouth and I stooped over to check the bottom desk drawer. Manila files were tucked into goose-poop-colored hanging folders. Most of the paperwork was invoices for various barge supplies. Nothing suspicious. I slammed the drawer shut. The metal of the drawer face hit the desk, and a muffled thunk sounded inside. I stared at the drawer a moment, and then tugged it open again. This time I reached in and dragged all the files toward me. On the bottom of the drawer, beneath the files, two VHS video tapes lay side by side. Each had a handwritten label. The first one read *Sonja Sucks* and the second *Lovin' Lavonne*.

Rocky's Ms. Lavonne, perchance? More stuff the cops must have decided wouldn't be of any use to them. Unless, of course, the cops were simply inept. As Eddy often said, you never know.

I held up the two tapes. "Check it out. Kinky really entertains himself on the job."

Eddy peered at the video cassettes in my hand, and Coop sidled over next to me. He took one of the tapes and flipped it end to end. "Let's see what's on them." He popped one into the VCR and hit play. We watched the gray snow fade and be replaced with the grainy image of a woman kneeling on a loveseat while a man with a very white, hairy ass went to town behind her.

Eddy gasped and clapped a hand over her eyes.

Coop laughed, and then the sound died in his throat. He walked closer to the monitor. "Isn't that the loveseat … in here?" He pointed to the piece of furniture in question.

Without a doubt, it was identical.

Coop cleared his throat, eyes glued to the action. "That's Kinky. Jesus. And I think that's Lavonne Smith—Ms. Lavonne—bingo player extraordinaire. And obviously, woman of questionable morals."

Disbelief and repulsion fought for priority on his face. "God, I can't believe I've actually sat on that nasty couch."

Eddy said, "Hey, wait a minute. If that's this office, where's the video camera?" We surveyed the room without seeing any indication of a camera.

The entire length of the loveseat and the front edge of the desk were caught in the frame. I walked over to the two posters hanging on the wall opposite the love seat and lifted the first one off its hook. Underneath was smooth, nicotine-colored sheetrock.

Coop came over and pulled Kinky's portrait off the wall. Sure enough, a tiny hole had been drilled though the plaster behind it. Coop turned the poster over. Another hole went straight through Kinky's right eyeball.

"Oh God, that is so wrong," I said, my lip curling in disgust.

"Figures. What a slime ball." Coop gingerly placed the picture back on its hook.

Eddy said, "What's on the other side of that wall?"

Coop frowned, and rubbed his chin, fingertips scraping against whiskers well past a five o'clock shadow. "A utility room that isn't used."

"Handy. Let's go have a peek." I headed for the door, gingerly stepping over the hole in the carpet.

"You two go on," Eddy told us. "I'll keep on checking out this damn mess."

I followed Coop out of Kinky's office while Eddy muttered under her breath about kinky bastards.

The storage room, no bigger than a bedroom closet, held a crusty mop, a stack of boxes, and a lot of cobwebs.

"This is the wall." Coop reached over and tapped on the sheet-rock behind the boxes.

"What's inside these?"

Coop sneezed as he pulled the top box down, dust floating around his head as he opened it. "Bingo paperwork, cashier stuff." He sniffed and looked up at the stack. "No place for a camera." He pulled another box down and set it aside.

I pulled the third one off the pile and realized it was much lighter than the other two. Sure enough, behind the box was the tiny hole that went through the wall into Kinky's office. I turned the box around. A cord snaked out the side and was plugged into an electrical socket in the wall. Another side of the cardboard had a perfect circle no more than an inch in diameter carved out of it.

Nestled inside, envelopes and assorted papers lay on top of a mini-camcorder that was secured to the cardboard with electrical wire and duct tape, its lens pressed against the hole in the side of the box. Another wire ran from the camcorder to a metal container the size of a couple of loaves of bread. The container was padlocked shut.

"Well, well, well," Coop said. "Kinky *was* making his own porn. It wasn't another urban legend after all."

I shuddered, lifted out the papers, and quickly sifted through them. There were a number of rumpled gas receipts and a business card for a storage warehouse off of Washington Avenue in Minneapolis. Interesting. If this stuff were hidden here, it must have some kind of significance.

One of the envelopes contained the title to a 1983 Caddy in Kinky's name. I'd seen the car in the Bingo Barge parking lot. The behemoth was all big tires, tinted windows, and curb feelers.

"He must have used his video-making hideout as some kind of safety deposit box," Coop said. I stuffed the business card and the gas receipts in my pocket and we put the rest of the boxes back. Coop carried the video equipment into Kinky's office. Eddy was still in Kinky's chair, in the act of carefully ripping off the top two pages of the big calendar on the desk.

"What are you doing?" I asked.

"Kinky's not going to miss these where he is. Might come in handy, never know. Could be secret codes in the doodles."

My hand shot out and stopped her in mid-rip. "Stop! What if the police need these for something? I'm sure they've already seen them. You can't take what's sitting here in plain sight. They'll know someone was here."

Eddy rolled her eyes at me. "Okay, you might be right. But what if one of those doodles holds the dirt we need?"

I raised an eyebrow at her.

"Fine. Anyway. I've decided I can't call that man by his given name after seeing his goods on the video. 'Kinky' damn sure fits the man." She nodded once emphatically. "So. What'd you find?"

Coop set the box on the desk. "The camcorder and probably a VCR." He fingered the padlock. Then he pulled out his keys and tried to fit each key into the slot on the bottom of the lock, but none of them worked.

I remembered the key ring in the desk drawer. "What about these?" I lifted out the ring I'd seen earlier and tossed it to Coop, who one-handed them in a jingle of metal. The third key he tried opened the lock with a soft click. Eddy and I crowded around as Coop lifted the lid. A tiny VCR occupied the box. I pulled it out and plugged the power cord into the wall.

"Ah, there's the power button," Coop muttered with satisfaction. A humming and a soft grinding came from the machine, and a video tape popped out. "And what do we have here?"

I grabbed the playing-card-sized cassette and turned it over and around. It was unlabeled, and the tape inside was at the start or had been rewound to the beginning. I walked over to the VCR, looked around for some kind of converter. The mini cassette slid into a VCR-sized doohickey that sat next to the player. I popped the carrier into the VCR and pressed play. Familiar gray snow filled the monitor. Then the picture, although still fuzzy, cleared up enough to show Kinky's loveseat. No one was in the frame. I pushed the fast-forward button. Pretty soon Kinky speed-walked in and disappeared behind his desk. A couple of long minutes of nothing passed. Then a scruffy-looking man popped in, made some animated movements, and zoomed out of the room.

Coop crossed his arms. "That was Buzz. Buzz Riley." A name on Rocky's list.

The tape kept zinging along. Pretty soon Kinky left and then returned, followed by Lavonne of *Lovin' Lavonne*. They chatted some, then moved over to the loveseat and proceeded to reenact the scene we'd already witnessed.

Thanks to fast-forward, they finished quickly, then resituated their clothes and stood discussing something. Lavonne appeared mad as a wet cat when she stormed out.

I said, "You don't think this is from the night Kinky was killed, do you?"

Coop said, "If I show up, you know it is."

Kinky popped in and out of the picture a few more times, and then another woman appeared, who, thankfully, kept her clothes on. She and Kinky exchanged words.

"God, I wish this thing had sound," I said.

The woman, obviously agitated, waved a finger with a long, blood-red polished fingernail at Kinky. "That's Rita Lazar," Coop said.

Rita and Kinky soon exited.

The tape zipped forward, and Coop flashed onto the screen. He buzzed around the room. At one point he had the legendary, bronzed bingo dauber, tossing it back and forth from one hand to the other. Kinky appeared again, followed by a few moments of very animated discussion. Kinky's arm went up, a finger pointing to the door. Coop set the dauber on the desk and exited.

"Man, that hurts almost as much the second time around," Coop said with a grimace.

We'd been standing mesmerized in front of the monitor for several minutes. Suddenly, we were jolted back to reality by the loud sound of shattering glass.

FIVE

I DOVE FOR THE light switch. Coop hit the power on the TV and frantically jabbed at the eject button on the VCR. Eddy stood rooted to the floor. Her eyes went wide and round, the whites showing bright against her dark skin.

"What the hell?" Coop whispered. With a rattle and click of the VCR, Coop yanked the cassette out of the player.

It had sounded as if the crash came from the main bingo floor. I whispered, "Where does this hallway go?"

"Past the restrooms and break room. There's an emergency exit at the end, but it'll set off the alarm."

I grabbed Eddy's arm. "Come on."

At the threshold, I stopped. Whoever broke in had to hear the hammering of our hearts. We were probably twenty feet away from the main bingo area, and I caught a brief flash of light. It blinked out as fast as it came on, followed by another loud bang.

"Shut the fuck up," a man said in an ominous, low voice.

Cops wouldn't break in, so who were these guys?

I dragged Eddy out the door, and Coop followed us. We hustled farther down the hall away from the bingo floor. A door was propped open, and I darted into the room as fast as one can dart with two people in tow.

Eddy flung herself against the wall. I knelt next to the doorframe, struggling to quiet my panicked breathing.

"Oh God," Eddy whispered, realizing which room we'd landed in from the acrid odor heavy in the air. "I don't want to die in the toilet. Is this the men's toilet? I'd rather die in the women's."

"Hush!" I poked Eddy with my elbow. She fell silent. My breath stuck in my lungs as footsteps echoed nearer. The interlopers had entered the hallway.

"The office is somewhere here," the low voice said.

"It damn well better be. Your directions are shit, Pudge," said another voice, accented and not as deep. Brooklyn, or Jersey, maybe? "Christ. I can't believe you did that, you dumbass."

Another oath from the first man. "I said I was sorry. Bastard shouldn't have done what he done. That's serious shit, ya know?"

"Yeah, yeah, what-the-fuck-ever. There's gotta be something here that'll tell us where those fucking nuts went." The footsteps stopped, fortunately not in front of our hideout. Probably at the office we'd vacated. "You should have at least made him tell you where the stupid truck is before you did him."

Nuts? I pressed my head hard against the tile wall, praying they wouldn't come closer, wondering what kind of nuts would have anything to do with the Bingo Barge and Kinky's death.

"Here, Boss," Pudge said.

I hazarded a quick peek around the doorframe. The light in Kinky's office blinked on. I jerked my head out of the line of sight.

Eddy leaned toward me. "We need a diversion to get the hell off this tub."

"What do you suggest?" Coop whispered.

"Shh." I waved a hand at them as the strange voices carried down the hall to us.

"…the hell is this? Some kind of fucking VCR?" asked the Boss.

"I dunno, Boss." Silence reigned momentarily, and then Pudge said, "What's on that tape?" More silence. I imagined one of them starting the *Lovin' Lavonne* cassette.

After what felt like a very long silence, Pudge said, "Holy shit, it's Stanley and some ho."

"And they're getting it on," the other man said. A pause, then, "Where's the cam?"

"I think this thing is it, Boss," Pudge said. The men went silent, and then metallic banging echoed down the hall.

"There's a goddamn camera set up so Stanley can get his rocks off watching replays of him banging someone? How long does the damn thing run? Is there a tape in it?" More pounding.

"Vincent, there's no tape in that machine." Pudge's voice pitched up an octave.

"Well, where did it go? If a tape was running when you were in here—oh Christ, Pudge. Do *not* tell me you're on camera smashing Long Dong Anderson's skull in. Why does this happen to me? All I want are my fucking nuts back! There's got to be some record of what that rat did with them. If I have to tear this goddamn place apart…" Vincent's voice had begun quietly and ended in a bellow.

"What if the cops have it?" Pudge dared to interject.

"You better hope they don't fucking have it. Keep hunting."

Almost as one, Coop, Eddy, and I shifted away from the doorway. The two strange men themselves were fucking nuts. We needed to get out of there before this Vincent, aka the Boss, and Pudge decided they had to take a leak.

Coop leaned into Eddy and me. "I have an idea," he whispered. "Three of us won't make it past the office door without being seen. But I think I can. I'll sneak out onto the floor and turn on the speaker system and the bingo machine. It's loud, and I'll stick the microphone close to the balls. It'll almost sound like gunfire. Then I'll head out the front doors. You guys do the emergency door. When you hear guns, run!" Coop scooted around Eddy and me. "Wish me luck," he said quietly, and slipped out the door.

Eddy and I peeked around the doorjamb to watch. As Coop closed in on the office, I saw he'd stuck the tape in his jacket pocket and it was dangerously close to tumbling out. I wanted to warn him, but Vincent and Pudge would hear me. He passed Kinky's office. As he moved into the shadows, the tape fell to the floor with an incredibly loud clatter.

After that, everything was a blur. Coop scrambled to grab the tape. His foot inadvertently bumped it, sending it skittering down the floor ahead of him. Two shadowy figures raced out of the office. The rubber on Coop's tennis shoes made desperate squeaking sounds on the cracked linoleum. He propelled himself from the hallway and into the bingo area, the two men tearing after him.

Eddy and I took off like spitballs out of a straw. She hit the emergency release on the door with the heel of her hand and we fled through the opening. Sirens screeched, slamming into my ears with the force of a physical assault. Red lights mounted beneath the walkway roof flashed bright.

A secondary gangway led from the barge, landing at the back of the boat very near where we'd boarded. A SUPPLIES ONLY sign was attached to the railing next to it. Eddy and I were over the supply bridge in a flash.

We crossed the road and ducked into a thick stand of trees between the barge and the lot we'd parked in. I pulled up short, grabbed a tree trunk for support, and struggled to catch my breath.

"You okay?" I gasped.

Eddy nodded, her cheeks puffing as she blew out air. "Where's Nicholas?"

Sirens still blared from the barge, and the red lights strobed, but we saw no other people. No Coop. No bad guys.

"Come on, child, we need to haul ass out of here."

I stumbled after Eddy. Real police sirens sounded in the distance, urging us to move our keisters. We burst out of the woods and climbed into Eddy's truck.

"Where the hell is Coop?" Near the barge, the silhouettes of a short, chubby figure and a taller, heavy-set man scrambled away from the barge. They ran across the street, jumped into a parked car, and rocketed off down the road.

"Boy's on his own now. Pray." With that, Eddy put the truck in reverse, hit the accelerator, and executed a textbook one-eighty. She slammed the gearshift into drive and jammed the pedal home.

As the truck's wheels won the fight and gripped asphalt, a lone figure careened out of the woods at a dead run and launched himself headlong into the bed of the pickup. The truck swayed with the sudden weight as Eddy peeled out of the lot. I twisted around, fingers digging into the headrest.

Coop's arm stuck straight up out of the bed of the truck, the videotape clutched triumphantly in his hand.

———

How we made it home in one piece, I have no idea. Coop disappeared the moment Eddy pulled the truck in the garage. I followed Eddy into the kitchen and watched as she spiked hot chocolate with a liberal splash of peppermint schnapps and we regrouped around the table in the loft.

"Thanks for making me ride in the back the whole way home," Coop said once he settled in.

"I wasn't about to stop just to let you in the cab. What if those bums were right behind us? No, sir. Once we were cruising, I wasn't stopping!" Eddy pursed her lips and shook her head. "How on earth did you manage to get away from that mess, Nicholas?"

I sipped my cocoa. The hot chocolate was laced with so much booze that it made me shudder, and heat oozed down my chest like lava.

"I got a hold of that damn tape and made a mad dash for the front doors. Those two wackos came racing out after me. I crossed the gangway, and then there was this huge crash behind me. Both of them were down flopping around on the dock like catfish in the bottom of a boat. The dude in the front must've hit one of the warped planks on the dock and tripped them both up." He eyed Eddy. "I thought you were gonna leave me in the dust there for a minute, Lead Foot."

Eddy's face crinkled, threatening a smile. "You ain't seen nothing yet, kid."

Coop turned on the 12-inch TV, fed the cassette into the VCR, and once again watched the hard-won tape on fast-forward. After Coop exited the office, nothing happened for what felt like many long minutes.

My eyeballs were drying out from staring at the screen. I forced a blink as Kinky entered the scene and disappeared from the shot, presumably sitting down behind his desk.

"There! Stop the tape!" I nearly tipped my chair over lunging for the VCR. Coop beat me to it and pressed the play button. The picture slowed down to real time.

A hefty man with a rotund belly appeared. Dressed in a black jacket and dark pants, he stood facing the desk. Gesturing wildly, his arms flapped like a bird's. Kinky sauntered into the picture again and leaned against the edge of his desk, a cajoling look on his face. The man took a step away from Kinky, and then Kinky's face changed, going from placating to lewd. In the blink of an eye, Kinky reached out and grabbed one of the man's butt cheeks and gave it a healthy squeeze. The side of the man's face turned deep red.

The next action occurred so fast that it was hard to make out. The fat man stiffened for a moment, lunged out of the frame, and then popped back in, one arm swinging in an arc toward Kinky. In a glint of gold, then a splatter of red, Kinky collapsed to the floor like a giant sack of potatoes. The man froze and stared a moment at the oversized, bronzed bingo dauber. He tossed the bloodied dauber to the ground, turned, and bolted out of the room. We watched the tape to the end, but there was nothing else either incriminating or indecent on it.

Coop pushed the stop button and we sat in stunned silence.

I finally croaked, "Holy crap." We had just witnessed the murder of another human being. I could hardly believe it. The man was a pig, but still. In a moment, in a flash, life could end. Just like that. I swallowed hard.

"Sweet Jesus, indeed. That man is a murderer." Eddy shuddered. "That has to be Pudge. Sweeeeeeeet Jesus," she repeated in a whisper.

"What the hell is going on?" I asked quietly. This was way out of our league. Oh hell, it was out of our league the moment Coop pulled me into the garage and told me what was going on. We needed to turn this mess over to Detective Bordeaux.

Eddy summarized, "Pudge killed Kinky. He was definitely one of the men on that floating palace of porn tonight. And Vincent wants his effing nuts." Eddy's lip twitched in distaste. "I certainly won't forget that man's foul mouth."

Coop held a thumb up. "We have Kinky's murder on tape." He added his forefinger to his thumb. "Kinky was taping his nooners with a secret camera in his office. Let's see. My prints are on the murder weapon." Up went his middle finger. "The man who conked Kinky appears with another crazy man named Vincent, while we're searching Kinky's office." Coop studied his hand. "These two yahoos are searching for some 'fucking nuts' and it seems Kinky did something with said nuts."

"Why are these nuts such a big deal?" I asked, unable to fathom why anyone would be concerned about nuts. The idea was preposterous. "Besides, what does it matter anymore? We have the tape and it shows that Coop's innocent."

Eddy ignored me. "One of them said something about a missing truck. What truck?" The mystery element of this mess had grabbed her very susceptible imagination.

I said, "What kind of nuts could throw these guys into such a tizzy?"

"I surely don't know. But Shay's right. We have a tape that clearly shows Coop didn't kill Kinky. We'll turn it over in the morning. No use in raising hell this late." Eddy stifled a yawn and stood. "My brain's had all it can handle. Nicholas, you tuck yourself in here one more night."

I peered at my watch. It was three o'clock in the morning. "Give me the tape, Coop. I'll call Detective Bordeaux in the morning."

SIX

I FELT LIKE I'D just closed my eyes when the alarm went off at nine. With a groan, I gingerly rolled out of bed, my muscles feeling the effects of the previous night's adventures.

PB&J toast in one hand and JT's card in the other, I walked into the living room. I plunked down on Ugly, the name Coop bestowed on my ragged couch, and dialed her number.

"Bordeaux," she answered, her voice gruff.

I swallowed and then said, "Hey JT. This is Shay O'Hanlon. From the Rabbit Hole."

"Oh, hi Shay." Her voice warmed a few degrees. "What's up?"

How much to tell her? I decided to keep it simple. "I've got something to talk to you about, and I wondered if you could swing by the café."

"Sure." There was a pause, and I imagined the detective checking her watch. "I can be there in less than an hour if that works for you."

"Yeah, that's perfect. Thanks."

I hung up and decided to see how Eddy was faring after our midnight exertions.

The old house was big, with the Rabbit Hole taking up almost half of the ground floor, and my apartment occupying the same space upstairs. Eddy had both stories at the rear of the building, and her lower level was connected to the Rabbit Hole kitchen by an ornate set of glass French doors. They had been installed as a divider when we remodeled to create the Hole space. The doors were usually closed and locked when she wasn't home. When Eddy was around, she liked leaving one of the doors open so she could easily stay in touch with the goings on at the Hole.

My footsteps echoed as I pounded down the stairs. I unlocked the French doors and called, "Eddy!" as I made my way through her living room into the kitchen. The scent of vanilla floated lightly in the air, and I opened her fridge to pull out a carton of milk.

"Eddy, you up?" I unfolded the top of the milk container and took a healthy hit. Coffee wasn't on. No enticing smell of bread crisping in the toaster wafted through the air. That was odd.

I ambled over to the stairs that were off the kitchen. "Eddy?" I strode back through the kitchen and living room, past the French doors with their gauzy cream curtains, and into the Hole. She wasn't in the kitchen or the back storage room, and she wasn't out front.

Kate stood next to the espresso machine, measuring out coffee beans.

"Have you seen Eddy this morning?" I asked.

"Nope."

"Thanks." I gave her a wave and jogged back through Eddy's kitchen and up her stairs, fear running through my veins. Be okay, I chanted to myself. She shouldn't have come with us last night. We'd probably caused the heart attack I'd been obsessing about.

Eddy's partially open bedroom door came into view. I prepared myself for the sight of her lifeless body lying on the bed. What if she was sprawled on the floor instead? What if she'd struggled to get up and couldn't? What if she died all alone? The thunderous thoughts in my brain came to a screeching halt as I pushed the door all the way open and saw Eddy's bed was empty. The sheets were rumpled, and the blanket lay half on the floor, but the bed was Eddy-free. This wasn't right. She never left her bed unmade.

I flew into the attached bathroom and was back in the bedroom in a blink. It occurred to me that maybe she'd gone up to see Coop. Of course! My heart shifted out of high gear, and the roaring in my ears lessened. Still, I shot down the stairs, out of the house, and into the two-car garage. Eddy's yellow pickup was still parked where we'd bailed out of it last night.

"Coop," I hollered up at the ceiling. "Coop!" I grabbed the broom and hammered on the wall. "Coop!"

The trap door opened, and Coop appeared. "Where's the fire?"

"Eddy. You haven't seen her, have you?"

"Eddy?" Coop's voice was gravelly from sleep and probably too many smokes.

"Yes, Eddy, for Christ's sake. She's gone!"

"Gone? What do you mean, gone?"

"Get down here!" My heart sped up so fast I feared it might slam its way through my ribs. I hoped I wouldn't pee my pants.

Coop's head disappeared, then he tossed a shirt, a pair of socks, and his shoes to the garage floor and scrambled down.

"Come on." I gathered up his clothes, and he followed me toward the house, wearing only his jeans.

"Man," he said, hurrying to keep up with me. "It's freezing out here. Could use a smoke, too."

I threw him a disgusted glare. "Your fatal attraction will have to wait."

We plowed into the kitchen, and I dumped Coop's clothing on the table.

"Shay, how do you know something's wrong?"

"Eddy, I told you. She's not here, and her bed's not made."

Coop would have done a good job of rolling his eyes if he'd been able to open them wide enough. "Who makes their bed anymore?"

"Eddy, you nincompoop. She always does. Always."

Coop peered at me as if I was a one-eyed frog. "Maybe she went out. Met up with one of the Knitters."

"I don't think so. Something feels wrong."

"Okay, okay…" He picked up his t-shirt from the table and pulled it over his head. He paused with one arm in the air and the shirt halfway on. "What's that?"

"What's what?"

Coop picked up a folded slip of paper from the table, half hidden under his socks. He read it, and I watched his face drain of color.

"What *is* it?"

He handed me a piece of lined paper, one edge jagged where it had been ripped out of a notebook. The words were scrawled in block letters:

GIVE US THE TAPE. AND THE NUTS.
YOU GET THE OLD LADY BACK IN ONE PIECE.
OR ELSE! CALL THIS NUMBER 908-555-9745
PS NO COPS OR SHE'S DEAD!!!!

My hands shook as I read the note again. Unfortunately, the words didn't change.

"Oh my god," Coop whispered.

I dropped the note as if it were contaminated and watched it drift down to the table. Hands clenched in my hair, I paced around the kitchen. "Okay. Okay. Calm. We need to stay calm." My voice rose a number of octaves. "Coop—oh God, we don't have any nuts."

"But we do have the tape."

"Yeah, we—oh my God, no!"

"What?" Coop half-stood, alarmed.

"The tape. I called JT, and she's going to be here—" I twisted my wrist and looked at my watch, "any minute."

"You tell her why you wanted to see her?"

"No. I just said I wanted to talk."

"Then you're going to go talk to her," Coop said reasonably. "Get rid of her fast and then come back so we can make that call."

"But what am I going to say I wanted to see her for? I can't tell her what's going on. I can't give her the tape. They wrote right on the note 'no cops' ..." I blinked hard and swallowed.

"Shay, I know." Coop's voice was remarkably calm. "Make a move on her or something. Tell her you're hot for her. Tell her—"

"Shay! Hey, Shay, you've got company!" Kate's shout from the entrance of Eddy's living room interrupted Coop mid-sentence.

As the milk I'd snitched from Eddy's fridge curdled in my stomach, I wished I'd been in the drama club in high school.

Coop sat immobile, his eyes wide and locked on mine.

"Shay!" Kate hollered again.

"I'm coming," I yelled back, unable to break Coop's gaze.

Coop jerked his head toward the door. "Go. You can do this."

I shut my eyes, breathed deep, and headed for my sixty seconds of fame.

Detective Bordeaux sat in the chair I'd lounged in the day before, steam curling from the cup she held. I approached her, a forced smile on my lips, no clue about what to say. She caught my gaze as I sat down across from her and returned my smile, faint laugh lines crinkling at the corners of her eyes.

"Thanks for swinging by, Detective." My voice was steadier than I thought it would be.

"My, we're formal this morning," she said, the tone of her voice teasing. "So what can I do for you?"

Oh, I don't know, maybe forget I called you this morning and go away? "I wanted to see if you'd heard anything about Coop or had any updates on the murder."

Her smile slackened, and the hard cop returned. She studied me silently for a moment. "Nothing on Coop. But someone did stir up some excitement at the Pig's Eye Bingo Barge last night."

Air in. Air out. "Really?" I forced my eyebrows up.

"The barge was broken into."

I couldn't pull my gaze from hers. She had me mesmerized and it seemed as if she could see through each lie I uttered. JT brought the cup to her lips, her eyes still laser-locked on mine.

"Why?" I asked.

"Not sure. Nothing was taken that we can tell. But someone was looking for something. What exactly, I don't know. A few interesting pieces of equipment were left behind. And there had to be multiple people involved because three points of entry and/or exit were established. In fact," JT's eyes drilled me, "Mr. Cooper's security code was used to disable the alarm."

I sat petrified, unable to move, breathe, or think.

"The panic alarm was set off by someone leaving through an emergency door."

The temptation to confess almost overwhelmed me. I wanted to explain to her that we were trying to help Coop. Explain that a big fat man named Pudge killed Kinky, and that Eddy was missing—no—kidnapped, and I was terrified … until the words on that scrappy piece of paper replayed on the screen in my head. PS NO COPS OR SHE'S DEAD!!!!

I couldn't take that chance.

"I don't know anything about it." I looked away, guilt spreading like fire through me. I looked down at my hands clasped tight in my lap, then back up to JT, the guilt receding in the face of what I felt I needed to do.

JT shrugged and her face relaxed. When she wasn't the woman of ice, she was hot as hell. For a very brief, crazy, improper moment, I imagined melting that ice away, until JT jolted me back to reality. "Something is stirring out there. Rumors we're picking up, that the Bingo Barge is more than it seems."

I was dying to ask what rumors they'd been hearing, but I didn't want to raise any more suspicions. I wondered if she knew about the nuts. Or about what kind of nuts the nuts were. Peanuts? Walnuts? Macadamia nuts? Who cared about freaking nuts? And why was she telling me this?

"What's on your agenda once you leave here?" I asked, unable to stand another moment of uncomfortable silence.

JT carefully placed her cup on the coffee table in front of her. "Headed to the barge."

I was all out of things to say and momentarily considered Coop's suggestion. It might not be very appropriate, but it would certainly get her mind off the case for a few stunned minutes. I wondered what her lips would feel like and pondered if it was distraction I intended or if some genuine interest was going on in the midst of this craziness after all. Cripes, I needed to get my head together and my mind out of dangerous places.

JT's cell phone rang. She excused herself to answer it and wandered over to the picture window, her back to me as she listened to whoever was at the other end. She snapped it shut. "I'm sorry to run, but we have a break in another case."

Oh, thank you, Lord. "Good news, I hope?"

"I hope so, too. Have a good day." She turned and called to Kate, "Thanks for the coffee." JT exited amid the sound of bells chiming against glass. The jingle was usually welcoming, but now it sounded starkly ominous.

———

Coop slowly paced around the kitchen table, phone clutched in his hand. "How'd it go?" he asked.

"About as well as expected. I'm sure JT thinks I've got a few loose screws."

"Did you take my suggestion?"

I narrowed my eyes at Coop. "No, I did not." I took a breath. "To be perfectly honest, I did think about it for a moment, no thanks to you."

"What'd I do?"

"You planted the seed. Oh, never mind that now—we have to make that call. You want to do it?"

"No way," he said as he lowered himself into a chair. "What if I say the wrong thing and piss them off?"

"Give me the damn phone."

He handed me the cordless, still warm from his hand. I took a very deep breath and punched the handwritten numbers into the keypad. One ring, and then another. I squeezed the handset so hard I was surprised it didn't crack in half. At last someone answered with a rude, "What?"

I swallowed the lump in my throat. "Hi," I said, not sure what to say to a kidnapper. "I, ah, we're calling about Eddy."

"'Bout goddamn time. We want that video and the truckload of nuts if you want the biddy back." Eddy yelled and cursed in the background. The sound of a hand being held over the receiver echoed in my ear, and I heard a muffled, "I can't hear, Boss," and then the man was back. At least Eddy was still kicking.

"We don't have any truck or the nuts."

"What ya mean you don't have the nuts?" The hand on the receiver returned, and the voice, again muffled but understandable

71

said, "Vincent, she says they don't have the nuts." There was more indecipherable murmuring in the background and a deep sigh came through the receiver. "We get the tape and the fucking nuts, and you get the pain-in-the-ass old broad."

"I told you, we don't have any nuts."

The man again spoke to Vincent. Faintly I heard Vincent say, "For Christ's sake, Pudge, gimme the fuckin' phone."

A couple of seconds went by and a new voice came on the other end. Vincent. I recognized his voice from the barge. "I don't know who the hell you are and I don't care. But you were on that blasted bingo pit last night. We saw you hot-wheel out of there in that old junker—and we followed you. You have a videotape we need, and if you have the tape, you must know something about the nuts."

"But we don't—"

"I know you ain't the cops, or you wouldn't have been creeping around that floating piece of crap. Kinky knew where that truck was, but he's dead and can't tell me where my fuckin' nuts are. You, however, are not dead … yet. So, see, you're gonna deliver 'em to us."

"But—"

"But nothin' lady. I need those nuts. And Pudge needs that tape. And the more I listen to that old lady bitch, the crankier I get. I want the nuts and the videotape or we'll take the broad apart piece by piece. After we stick some duct tape on her mouth, of course."

"But how—I don't—" Stall them Shay, come on! In a breath I said, "I need more time."

"Jesus. You got till tomorrow. Call this number at one o'clock. Not a moment later. I'll tell you where to meet us with the goods. Understand?"

"Yeah, but—"

"Listen, lady, don't screw with me. Get me my nuts and that damn tape." Vincent hung up.

Silence filled the kitchen. Coop stared at me expectantly, and when I didn't say anything, he waved a big hand in front of my face. "Earth to Shay, what'd they say?"

I mechanically pushed the off button on the keypad before the ungodly "if you would like to make a call" chant began, and set it gently on the tabletop. I gave him the rundown. Coop slumped in his chair and ran a hand through his hair. "How are we supposed to come up with these stupid nuts?"

"Beats me. Why do they think we have the nuts? Nuts... peanuts?" I said.

"Almonds?"

"How about cocktail nuts?"

"Or mixed nuts?"

"Walnuts?"

"Cashews. They're my favorite."

I smiled for a moment in spite of it all. "They know we were sneaking around the barge. And we have the tape they want. I suppose they figure we're part of whatever Kinky was involved in."

"Maybe we should tell Detective Bordeaux."

"Are you crazy? You know what they said they'd do to Eddy. No way. We can't take that chance, Coop." I sent him a sideways look. "Since when do *you* want help from the law?"

73

Coop shook his head. Silence reigned as we attempted to wrap our brains around the latest turn of events. Coop finally took a deep breath. "You know, Rocky is always around the barge, in the back, being sent off by Kinky on this errand or that job."

"So?"

"He's got, like, a photographic memory. He can see someone or hear a name, and months later he can pull it out of that mind of his as if he heard it yesterday. Maybe he heard Kinky talking about the nuts. I'll come with you this time. I didn't kill Kinky, and we have the proof."

SEVEN

We rolled into Rocky's neighborhood a little after eleven o'clock in the morning. We knew Rocky didn't get out during the day much, but we couldn't really postpone looking for him. I drove, wondering what would happen to Rocky now that there would be no more errands to run for Kinky. Coop kept lookout for Rocky's green down coat. I hoped we were far off of Detective Bordeaux's radar. I'd promised the detective I'd let her know if I saw our fugitive, and it wouldn't look good trying to explain what he was doing in my truck.

After crisscrossing the streets, searching likely corners, and striking out everywhere, we gave up. I parked in front of Rocky's boardinghouse, and we headed for the entryway. The building it-self was an ancient, two-story house. The faded wood siding was in dire need of a new coat of paint, and the porch steps sagged dangerously underfoot.

The foyer held a bank of six silver mailboxes, and a set of warped stairs led to the second floor.

Coop scoped out the boxes. "He's upstairs, 2C."

"Cross your fingers he's home."

The upper floor was as worn out as the ground level. The walls were dingy white, and the carpet beneath our feet was threadbare. The air was heavy with the smell of fried hamburger and onions. We found 2C, and Coop rapped on the door. No response. He knocked again, and this time we heard a voice from within yell, "No one home."

"Rocky, it's me, Shay, and Coop's with me. Can we talk to you?"

Silence. Then he yelled again, louder, "No one home!"

"Rocky," I leaned my forehead against his door. "We'd like to ask you a couple things." Nothing.

I raised my eyebrows at Coop and mouthed, "What now?"

Coop grinned wickedly. "Hey buddy, it's Coop. How about some Popeye's?"

Another long silence. Coop was about to knock again when the door swung open. Rocky stood before us, his green jacket drowning him, his aviator hat pulled low over his eyes. "I am ready for Popeye's, Nick Coop and Shay O'Hanlon."

———

We sat down with our food as the lunch rush hit, and I ate my first real meal in two days. Rocky still had a pile of food on his plate long after Coop and I had depleted ours.

Coop sighed the sigh of a man with a happy belly and said, "Shay and I have a couple things we'd like to ask you, Rocky."

His bushy eyebrows wiggled. "What kind of questions do you want to ask me, Nick Coop?"

"You remember what happened to Mr. Stanley, right?"

Rocky's eyes got big, and the whites of his eyes gleamed. He nodded solemnly. "Yes, Nick Coop. I remember what happened to Mr. Stanley."

Coop looked at me again, calmer, and then returned his gaze to the rotund man. "We're trying to figure out who would want to hurt Mr. Stanley."

Rocky stared benignly at Coop with those wide eyes.

My turn. "Did you hear Mr. Stanley talking to anyone about some kind of, um, nuts?"

One eyelid drooped slightly as Rocky's eyes shifted to meet mine. I was trying to think of something else to ask that might actually elicit a response when he said, "Mr. Stanley was on the phone all the time."

We waited for him to say more, but nothing was forthcoming.

Coop asked, "Did you hear Mr. Stanley on the phone talking about a shipment of nuts?"

I sucked air through my straw as we waited for Rocky to chew twenty-six times. He really did, and I know because I counted. He swallowed and said, "Mr. Stanley told me to never repeat what I heard when he was on the phone talking about the nuts."

Whoa. He had heard of the nuts. Begin Project Information Extraction. Coop leaned forward. "What did you hear Mr. Stanley say about the nuts?"

Rocky said very quietly, "Mr. Stanley told me to never say anything about the nuts to anyone or he'd knock my block off."

"Hey," I said softly, "Mr. Stanley can't hurt you now. Coop's in trouble, and so is another friend of ours. We need to find out about these nuts so we can help both of them. Can you help us help them?"

The muscles in Rocky's cheeks bulged in and out as he rhythmically clenched his teeth. Then he rubbed his right eye and said, "I don't want anything bad to happen to Nick Coop or your friend."

Lord, this was an exercise in patience. What I really wanted to do was grab the puffy lapels of Rocky's jacket and shake some answers out of him. "You might be able to help both of them if you tell us what you heard about the nuts."

"Okay, Shay O'Hanlon. I will try. But I was not listening on purpose."

"That's okay. Sometimes we just hear things. We want to make sure that the people who are innocent don't get in trouble, too."

Coop added, "It's really okay to tell us what you heard. Did you hear Mr. Stanley on the phone talking about the nuts more than once?"

"I heard Mr. Stanley talk to someone exactly three times about the nuts, Nick Coop."

"What did you hear when Mr. Stanley talked about the nuts?" I asked.

Rocky scrunched his eyes. Crow's feet fanned out, reminding us that although Rocky sounded like a child, he wasn't. "Mr. Stanley said, 'Hello. Yeah, I know I owe you one. No, I'll make good on my word. What do you want? When's the truck rolling in? No, no—I—What's it carrying? Nuts? What do you mean nuts? Almonds? What is that? Oh. No. How long? Okay. Bye.'"

It took me a minute to realize Rocky was repeating verbatim what he'd heard Kinky say on the phone. The effect was unsettling.

"Was that the end of the conversation?" Coop asked.

"Yes, Nick Coop."

I figured that if he could pull a date out of that priceless brain of his, we'd be able to put together a timeline. "Do you remember when this conversation took place?"

"It was eleven days, three hours," Rocky tugged the sleeve of his jacket up and peered at a large watch attached to his wrist, "and fourteen minutes ago, Shay O'Hanlon."

Holy shit.

Coop's vocal abilities returned before mine did. "Do you know who was sending the almonds to Mr. Stanley?"

"Mr. Stanley said one name exactly five times when he talked about the truckload of nuts. Then he also talked about the truckload of 'stupid nuts' to a bingo lady."

Thank God Kinky overlooked Rocky. I suspected that Kinky often forgot that Rocky was more than a vehicle for errands and menial tasks. Mr. Word-For-Word had a comfortable position: under the radar but well within listening range.

"What names did you hear?" Coop gently asked.

"Mr. Vincent Ragozzi."

The elusive and threatening Vincent now had a last name.

"And Ms. Rita."

That revelation was a bombshell. Coop raised his eyebrows at me. "Do you know what Ki—Mr. Stanley was going to do with the nuts?"

I smiled weakly at Coop's near slip.

"You should always keep your tires inflated to the exact manufacturer recommendations printed on the tires of your vehicle."

I put a hand to my forehead and slid it over my face, concealing the smile I was unable to squelch. Rocky had done a good job of managing to stay with us. Now we were losing him to his mind's inner machinations.

Coop said with a grin, "I'll remember that. Did you hear where Mr. Stanley was going to store the nuts?"

Rocky nodded dramatically. "He was going to put them in Ms. Rita's storage warehouse, Nick Coop."

Coop said, "Do you know where this storage place is?"

Rocky's eyes shifted to the ceiling as he thought about it. "It is Lazar and Company Dry Storage, 1047 Washington Avenue Northeast, Minneapolis, Minnesota 55550."

I pulled a pen from my pocket and scrambled for something to write on. Rocky repeated the name and address for me and I scrawled it on an unused napkin. We sat quietly for a minute, processing the information our pal had coughed up. Then we asked Rocky about the other two conversations, but there wasn't anything critical in either one. However, before we brought him home, I wanted to run one more name by him.

"Rocky," I said, reaching across the table and giving his hand a squeeze to bring his attention to me. "You've done a great job. Now I have one more question."

He silently gazed at me, his golden eyes gleaming.

"When we talked last time, and you told me the names of the people who'd been angry when they'd spoken to Mr. Stanley. One of the names was Buzz Riley."

"I remember, Shay O'Hanlon."

"Why was Buzz Riley mad at Mr. Stanley?"

"I don't know. But he's a very mean man. He scares me."

Coop said, "I know he's scary. But he's not going to hurt you, okay?" He patted Rocky on the shoulder. "How do you know that Buzz was mad at Mr. Stanley?"

"Because Buzz Riley told Mr. Stanley, 'If you don't fork over the dough, I'm going to pop your eyeballs out and have them for supper.'"

We cleared the table, and Rocky suckered us into buying him two more orders of rice and beans, an order of fried chicken, a chocolate-strawberry shake, and large fries—all to go.

The return trip was a quiet one. Rocky hopped out, loot in hand, in front of his boardinghouse. He said, "I hope I helped you, Nick Coop, and your friend, too. Thank you for the most excellent food, Shay O'Hanlon." He took a couple of steps and then turned around to face us. "You should keep your house at a comfortable sixty-eight degrees for optimal energy usage and monetary savings."

———

I ran into the Hole shortly past two to grab a couple cups of emergency caffeine. I steamed milk and pulled two double shots of espresso. Kate eyed me as she put the finishing touches on a customer's order, concern shadowing her face. "Is there anything I can do?"

"No, just keep making the good detective her drink if she comes by again."

"Does this have something to do with Eddy?" Kate was quiet when she wasn't on the trail of some hot babe, but she was observant, and she watched the Rabbit Hole like a hawk. On any normal day, by this time, Eddy would have made at least one visit to the Hole to check out the latest happenings. Coupled with my panicked searching for her earlier and the rather tense visit with JT, it didn't take a nuclear physicist to fill in the blanks.

I didn't dare tell Kate the entire story. She couldn't do anything to help, and although I trusted her implicitly, her love of gossip scared me. She might slip up and say something to someone. Someone like Detective Bordeaux. After quick deliberation I said, "Kate, something *is* going on. But I can't talk about it yet." With much more confidence than I felt, I added, "But everything's going to be okay."

She squinted at me for a moment longer, and then placed the mugs of coffee she'd been doctoring up on a tray and set off to deliver them.

I sighed deeply, finished the drink prep, nabbed a half-full box of glazed donuts from the kitchen, and hustled everything out to the loft. Coop sent down a bucket on a rope for the cups and donuts, and the ladder for me.

We settled down with the goods.

I said, "We know now that the nuts Vincent wants back are almonds. I didn't realize that almonds were a high-ticket item, did you?"

"Nope," Coop said as he chomped on another bite. "What can be so important about a bunch of almonds? Let's Google them. Go get your laptop."

I climbed down and ran over to the house to retrieve my laptop, happy that we'd installed high-speed wireless Internet in the Rabbit Hole a few months back. I hoped we were close enough to pull in the signal.

Sure enough, I fired up the laptop and jumped right onto Google. Coop hovered over my shoulder as I typed *almonds* in the search field. Almost instantly, the top ten of over six million hits appeared. I scrolled though the first page and realized we needed to narrow the field. I added the word *crime* to *almonds*, and that cut the amount of hits to half a million. The first read, Almonds: The New Gold. I clicked on the link.

> Almond and walnut growers in California are literally going nuts. A highly sophisticated band of nut-nappers have been coordinating break-ins at nut orchards statewide. Truckloads of nuts, each worth over half a million dollars, have been stolen. Rumors circulating indicate the thefts may have coastal Mafia connections. Sales of California nuts last year brought in a whopping $44 million. Sales are rising, making the nuts a hot commodity in more ways than one. Recent speculation holds the nuts are being shipped to markets overseas.

He said, "Kinky died over a truckload of almonds? I suppose stranger things have happened." He reread the article. "You know, Vincent and Pudge sound kind of like the guys on *The Sopranos*."

"Yeah." I shifted in my chair, draping an arm over the backrest to face Coop, who was still standing behind me. "You think Vincent and Pudge are a part of the mob?"

"Could be. Looks like the almond thing has that kind of connection."

"Holy crap. What if we got Eddy kidnapped by real live gangsters?" I closed my eyes. This could absolutely not be happening. The Mafia? Kidnapping? Murder? Whose life was this? It sure as hell couldn't be mine.

"Maybe we should go to Detective Bordeaux. I didn't kill Kinky. Maybe they didn't find my prints." A faint note of hope glimmered in his voice.

"No freaking way! Come on, if this really is the Mafia, they're apt to outfit Eddy in some cement shoes and force her to take a swan dive into the Mississippi if we don't give them what they want."

Coop sank into a chair and put his head in his hands. "You're right. We have to find those damn nuts in less than," he glanced at his watch, "twenty-four hours."

Heavy silence filled the room. "Okay," I said as I picked up a pen and began working the cap on and off. "We need to find out what Rita knows about this mess, and if she has any idea where the nuts are." I froze for a second, then pulled out all the junk I had stuffed into my pockets, dumped it on the table, and started sifting.

Coop cocked his head. "What're you doing?"

"Remember the card that was in the video box on the barge?" I finally found it and held it up. "This."

"Yeah?"

The front of the card read LAZAR AND COMPANY DRY STORAGE. The address matched the one Rocky had given us. "It verifies what Rocky said."

Coop took the card from me and flipped it over. Two lines had been written on the back side: *IN-Wednesday, November 17th* and *OUT-Monday, November 22nd*. Today was Friday the 19th, so the nuts weren't scheduled to be shipped out for at least a few days.

"Maybe that's the nutty timeline," Coop said. He grinned and returned the card.

I proceeded to tuck my pocket detritus away as I shook my head in exasperation. "A wiseass right up to the gritty end, aren't you? I think it's time we go check out that storage company."

"My thoughts exactly. But we better wait for it to get dark before we break in anywhere. I'm still a wanted man. I probably shouldn't have gone to Popeye's with you and Rocky."

"But you didn't get busted."

"Nope. And I don't want to chance it again if I don't have to."

I blew out a big gust of air and looked at my watch. It was 2:30, and we'd have daylight for at least another three hours. "How about if I see if I can have a word with Ms. Rita in the meantime. By the time I'm done with that, nightfall will be ours."

"All right." Coop pulled the laptop toward him, laced his fingers together, and twisted them inside out in a stretch. His knuckles popped and I cringed. "I'll see you in a little bit. I'm going to see what else I can find on stolen nuts. Good luck."

It dawned on me I had no idea where Rita Lazar lived. "Hey, Coop, what's Rita's address?"

"Guess that would help." His fingers flew over the keys. "Pig's Eye Bingo has a record of all patrons who've signed up for a Pig's Eye Club card. I cracked into that system after my first week."

In less than three minutes, Coop had Rita's address, Map-Quested it, and scrawled directions on a piece of paper. As I started my pickup and backed out of the garage, I caught sight of Eddy's old yellow jalopy. My heart twisted and my breath caught. Everything came down to the woman who was the world to me. "Don't worry, Eddy," I muttered under my breath as I sped down the alley, "everything's gonna be okay."

EIGHT

RITA LIVED IN TYROL Hills, a well-to-do neighborhood in Golden Valley. Houses were large, charming, and expensive, with peaked brown-shingle roofs and Swiss chalet windows. Wild ivy crept up white stone walls, the growth more brown than dark green now that the days had grown cooler. The sun shone through mostly bare tree branches, dappling the road in front of me. The streets were curvy and hilly, unlike the grid system of city blocks in Minneapolis.

I tried to follow Coop's hastily written directions and passed the same street sign for the third time. After a few more erroneous but scenic turns, I spotted the correct house number and pulled to the curb. The three-story house was huge, castle-sized. Arched windows framed with dark walnut colored wood looked like square, black eyes, intimidating and unfriendly. The yard was immaculate, the grass tenaciously hanging onto every last bit of summertime green, thanks to a rare mild fall in the northland. Expensive lawn ornaments were carefully arranged on its lush surface.

A shiny tan Audi sat in the driveway, and I hoped it belonged to Rita. I had little time to chase the woman down. From the appearance of her house and vehicle, she didn't seem like the type to haunt a rundown, blue-collar gambling boat. Maybe that's one way the rich got their kicks. Take a ride on the wild side, mix with the rabble.

I took a deep breath, stepped out of the truck, and cut across the lawn to the front door. The dense grass cushioned my steps. It had been mowed very recently, and I sucked in the earthy smell with a pang of end-of-warm-days-and-start-of-long-nights sadness.

The dark front door towered over me, all planks and black metal, coming to the same sort of peak that followed the style of the windows. The place was cold and medieval. It probably had a dark, moldy dungeon where visitors were regularly chained and beaten. Before I lost my nerve, I stabbed the doorbell and heard a melodious gonging within.

I was about to push the button again when the door swung open, revealing a short, small-boned woman dressed in a dark blue pantsuit and punishing pointed-toe high heels. Her black hair was swept up in a stylishly messy 'do that probably cost a month's utilities at the Rabbit Hole. Her skin was bronzed, but it was hard to tell whether she worshipped the electric sun bed, had just returned from some exotic location, or if the color was her natural skin tone. The showstopper was a huge brown and black speckled mole on her chin sprouting pitch-black whiskers. The monstrosity had to be the size of Rhode Island. I wondered why someone with so much money hadn't had the unsightly thing removed.

She regarded me with a mixture of curiosity and annoyance. She said in a controlled voice used to giving orders, "If you're here for the yard, the company's already sent someone."

"No, actually, I'm wondering if I could talk to Rita Lazar about the business she owns on Washington Avenue. My name is Shay O'Hanlon, and—" Uh oh. Fatal error. I hadn't thought of a passable reason for questioning her. Hastily, I babbled on. "I work for the Minnesota Storage Facility Inspector's Office, and we're working on coordinating the inspection of your commercial property for proper insurance, licenses, and a rodent-free building—ah, pest control, actually." As soon as *rodent-free* popped out of my mouth, I figured she'd see right through me and kick my butt right down the stately steps.

Instead, she said, "I'm Rita Lazar." Her narrow dark eyes peered at me through the frown on her otherwise smooth face. I pegged her for late forties, maybe older if she'd had a face lift, which was a distinct possibility since her eyes were slightly pulled at the corners, giving her a cat-like appearance.

She slowly extended a dainty hand with French-manicured nails. Her grip was cold and exactly what I imagined uncooked lutefisk would feel like. I released it quickly.

Rita took a step back, the clatter of her heels loud on the polished stone floor. "Come in, then," she said, her tone both regal and disdainful, as if she were allowing a contaminated serf into her august palace. I crossed the threshold, and Rita swung the door shut behind me.

I hurried to keep up as she strode across a foyer larger than my apartment and through a room that out-sized Eddy's two-car garage. The room was devoid of furniture and lined with empty, built-in walnut bookshelves. Nice library for a book lover, but too dark for my tastes. I wondered if she was redecorating or perhaps moving in or out.

Rita kept trucking, heels clacking like mini explosions, through to another room that adjoined the library. This room was as bare as the first. Indentations on an expensive Oriental rug looked like they may have come from a heavy table resting atop it.

I followed her into a nook that actually appeared lived in. Sunlight cast dusty beams through spotless floor-to-ceiling windows. A round table with four chairs was tucked in one corner. A wine-colored leather couch faced a gigantic flat-screen TV, and a recliner with a built-in vibration mechanism sat next to it. My stressed out muscles gave me an urge to give that hummer a try, but I figured Rita wouldn't be very happy to have a stranger playing with her gizmos.

Two paintings hung on the wall facing the window. I did a double take when I saw them. One was a black and white silhouette of the Minneapolis skyline, and the other was a rendering of the same skyline in full color, ablaze in a gorgeous sunset. "Nice paintings."

Rita waved a hand toward the couch, and I took a seat. "Yes, they're original Rodriguez. She's an up-and-coming local artist." Rita eyed my faded jeans, Nikes worn-down-at-the-heel, and maroon U of M sweatshirt with its frayed cuffs. "I doubt they're anything you'd be interested in."

Nice woman. She'd probably have a stroke if she knew that I not only considered Alexandra Rodriguez a good friend, but she had painted the interior of the Rabbit Hole, and we had a number of her pieces on display. I couldn't wait till I had a chance to tell Alex where some of her work was hanging.

Rita perched on a chair next to the table. "I hope you don't mind if I smoke." On the tabletop, a dinner-plate sized ashtray overflowed with cigarette butts.

I shrugged. I wasn't about to say anything combative to a woman from whom I needed answers.

Rita fired up and sucked in a lungful. She propped her elbow on the edge of the table, held the cigarette daintily between two fingers, and squinted at me through the smoke. "So what can I do for you?"

Showtime. "Ms. Lazar, we wanted to follow-up on some information that our office came across in the last couple of days." I kicked myself. At the very least, I should have thought to bring a clipboard or something that would make me come off even mildly official.

"And what information would that be?" she asked dryly, eyes flicking up to study the glowing end of her cigarette.

I was mesmerized by the quivering mole on her chin and had to force my gaze away, back to her squinty eyes. "We have information your facility accepted a load of California nuts, but your licenses don't allow for storage of foodstuffs."

Her manicured eyebrows arched delicately, and Rita took another long puff. She sucked so deeply and held the smoke in so long that I wondered if she was used to puffing a whole lot more than cigarettes. "I'm afraid you'll have to speak with my husband about that." As she spoke each word, fumes puffed out of her mouth.

So Rita was married. Ms. Rita was all I'd heard since Rocky had uttered her name. "Actually, what we're hoping to accomplish today is to secure permission to complete an inspection of the building, and then we can go ahead and issue a license for food storage." I surprised myself by coming up with such a realistic-sounding crock of shit.

Rita snorted, and then cleared her throat, like a baseball player getting ready to lob a snot ball. I barely contained a cringe. "The nuts aren't there anymore."

Not sure what to say to that, I simply nodded. I so loved sailing by the seat of my britches. "We understand the product is no longer there, but we could make the license retroactive, and then you'd be legal for that and any other shipments of nuts in the future. We'd also like to inspect the nuts, unless of course they've been shipped out of the state. Do you have any additional shipments coming in?" I was doing so well, I was on the brink of believing myself.

Rita scowled, as much as her botoxed features would allow. "I don't think there'll be any additional shipments. My husband and I are planning to move back to Portugal, where I'm originally from." She must have come from Portugal some time ago since I couldn't detect an accent. That also explained the reason for the empty rooms. "In fact," she added, "we're planning on leaving a week from now. So, if you don't have any other questions, I have to continue packing."

I thought folks in this neighborhood would have packers and movers taking care of such menial tasks. She stood, and I followed suit. "I do have one last question, Mrs. Lazar. Where did the nuts ship from your site?"

Rita stood still, and I watched her left eyelid twitch. "I don't know," she said, and her eye twitched again, and she touched a finger to it. "You'll have to ask Luther."

"That sounds like a good idea." I made a play of checking the time. "Where can I find him? It's running late, and I'd like to get this squared away as soon as possible."

"He should be at the Washington Avenue warehouse. We have a couple of other storage facilities, but I think that's where he's working today." Her eyes narrowed on me again. "You know, I don't think you showed me any credentials earlier."

Oh, shit. Trying to think fast, like the con artist I wasn't, I patted my waist and managed a weak, "It seems I forgot my ID card in the car. If you'd like to step outside with me, I can show it to you." Please don't, please don't, please don't.

"Yes, I think that's a good idea." With that, Rita turned and steamed out of the room with me hot on her tail, her still-burning cigarette forgotten in the ashtray. She charged into the foyer, and as she was about to open the fourteen-ton front entry, the deep, echoing gong of the doorbell sounded. She pulled the heavy door open, and three kids stood on her stoop, freshly scrubbed and looking as nervous as I felt.

A chubby boy with a red crew cut and smattering of freckles across his nose stepped forward and said, "*Hola*. We're part of the Burnside Middle School Spanish Club, and we're trying to raise money for a trip to Mexico in the spring and we've got ..." The kid droned on. I took the opportunity to slip around the group while they had Rita's attention.

As I hot-footed it to the truck, Rita shouted, interrupting the redhead who was still working on one of the longest sentences I'd ever heard. "Hey, you! Shag, Shaw, O'Hanly … whatever, I want your ID—"

Luckily Rita was trapped by the kids, who weren't budging off her front steps. They must have really wanted to go to Mexico. I hopped into the truck and quickly backed down the street and into a neighbor's drive, and turned my truck around. I mashed the pedal to the floor and beat hell out of there.

NINE

I DROVE THE SPEED limit home, not wanting to take the chance on getting pulled over. I thought about what Rita had told me, or maybe, more importantly, what she hadn't told me. That eye twitch thing was a dead giveaway that she was lying through her teeth. She knew damn well where the almonds were. What did it all mean?

Rocky told us about Rita and Kinky's confrontation, and I definitely saw a ruthless streak in that evil woman that I wouldn't want to tangle with. Could she be capable of murder? If she knew where the nuts were, that meant they really didn't disappear. Kinky thought the nuts were missing. But Rita had them. Vincent and Pudge obviously thought Kinky was in on the disappearance. I wondered if they knew about Rita. Hell, maybe Kinky was in cahoots with Rita and her husband. But what were Rita and hubby going to do with the nuts? Ransom? Maybe they were going to ransom the nuts to Kinky. But that would mean that Kinky wasn't involved with Rita and Luther after all. Jesus. The possibilities made my head spin.

Weariness from one too many shots of adrenaline was beginning to take its toll. I turned down the alley and pulled up to the garage behind the café. I pressed the button on the remote, and the old garage door rumbled up. The engine ticked softly as I climbed out of the pickup and banged the broom handle on the wall to get Coop to open up. I was about to push the wall-mounted garage remote to close the rolling door when a figure silhouetted itself against the deepening twilight outside. Detective Bordeaux. The hairs on the back of my neck stood up and I froze, a deer in the high-beams once again.

With the realization who was standing in the doorway, it dawned on my muzzy brain that Coop had to have heard my pounding. Was he in the process of opening the trap door? Thank the freaking heavens the entrance sat toward the back of the garage, in the deepest of shadows. Oh shit. The light from above would spill down into the darkness.

Rapidly I moved toward the good detective and said in a loud voice, praying Coop would hear, "Detect—uh, JT!" Play up to her, Shay. Do this.

My feet didn't slow when I came abreast of her—I strolled right past her out into the night. JT turned around, away from the open garage door and took a step to follow me. Either she hadn't seen anything that piqued her interest, or she was playing a very good game. I swung around the corner out of sight of the garage door. She followed like an obedient pooch and I resisted the urge to pat her on the head.

"So," I turned on her and said breathlessly, "what are you doing lurking in my alley?" The best defense was always a weak offense.

My alley-lurker bit garnered a half-smile, then the cranky expression on JT's face the day before returned with a vengeance. Not surprising in light of my strange actions. I wondered if her voice would come out smooth as butter or harsh and accusatory.

She said, "I was in chatting with Kate. She said you'd been gone most of the day, and that you're acting kind of weird, but she didn't really explain what that meant. But she indicated something wasn't quite right. I decided to wander around a bit and make sure everything's okay."

Kate was dead meat, just as soon as I could get rid of JT. "Kate's a bit high-strung. Everything's fine." I waved a hand at JT, hoped I sounded sincere. She was burning up what precious time Coop and I had to figure out what to do next. Desperation gripped my neck in a chokehold, and I shuddered.

JT saw me shiver and stepped closer, stopping less than an arm's length away. She was so close I could smell laundry soap on her clothes. Silent electricity popped inside me, and I wondered if she felt it as well. Loose strands of hair that had escaped her ponytail waved in the slight breeze. Her stern demeanor faded away, replaced with what looked like obvious concern. The dim light accentuated her cheekbones. She was a very beautiful woman when she wasn't scowling.

"What's going on, Shay?" JT asked softly. "What can I do to help?"

I really, really wanted her question to be an honest offer of assistance, but my paranoid state of mind prevented me from taking her words at face value. She gave me the impression she'd be very

good at using every trick in her cop psychology book to her benefit. But then again, maybe I was being a touch rash. She sure
sounded sincere. Oh hell. I hated it when people I tried to blow off
started being nice to me. Or at least pretended to be nice to me. It
was sorely tempting once again to dump the entire, sorry affair
into her lap. However, Vincent's warning bounced around my
brain like an irritating song I couldn't get rid of—call the cops and
it would be lights out for Eddy.

"JT, nothing's wrong, okay? I—" At that moment Coop walked
around the corner and stopped short of running into JT. His eyes
widened, his jaw dropped. So I did the only thing I could think of
to buy him some time to get away.

I grabbed JT and pulled her toward me, hard enough I felt the
whoosh of her breath as her body slammed into mine. I mashed
my lips on hers, surprised when she didn't immediately shove me
away. The element of surprise must have been in my favor. She
stood frozen, arched slightly away from me, but I kept my mouth
attached to hers. I peered desperately over her shoulder praying
Coop had disappeared. He was still there, the expression on his
face a mix of amazement and horror. I tried to pull JT tighter to
me when she grabbed a handful of my hair and jerked my head
back, exposing my throat, effectively ending the most interesting
and awkward kiss I'd ever had.

JT remained pressed against me, her breath warm against my
neck. Good thing she wasn't a vampire, or I'd have been dinner.
"Well." She whispered, paused, then repeated, "Well."

I smiled weakly, wondering if the roots of the hair tangled in
her fist were going to tear out of my scalp. The woman certainly
had power over me in more ways than one. Did cops fraternize

with people who may be involved in nefarious activity? I'd started this, but that didn't mean she couldn't exploit the situation. Was JT playing me, trying to strip my defenses so I'd confess my sins? Really—what did she know? She knew I was Coop's friend. That was it. That in and of itself wasn't a crime. She couldn't haul me in for that. Could she?

I cleared my throat and tried to look her in the eye but the angle was bad. "Ah, this is slightly uncomfortable."

JT loosened her grip so my head was only slightly tilted away from her. The icy glare was back. "Shay—" She looked away for a moment and then returned her gaze to my face. It seemed she was trying so hard to keep roiling emotions stuffed inside, but they were very close to bubbling over. "I'm not an idiot. I know something's going on here. I don't know you well, but my instincts rarely guide me in the wrong direction. Whatever it is, you're in it up to your pretty little ears. I—I really want to—help you." She released my hair and settled her hand lightly on my shoulder as she took a half-step back.

I broke our gaze like she'd broken our kiss—abruptly. That smooch was something I'd have to seriously consider when no one's life was at stake. That, and the fact she thought I had cute ears. I put a bit more distance between us, my hand momentarily covering my eyes. "I, ah—sorry about that." I squinted between my fingers. Thank God Coop was gone.

It was dark enough now that all I could make out were the angles and planes of JT's face. Easier talking to a shadow, anyway. I needed to play this very carefully. JT still could turn out to be a solid ally if things got desperate enough.

"It's like this," I began, not wanting to lie and not wanting to push her further away. Frustration festered, and I turned to the wall of the garage, biting my lip both figuratively and literally, my palms and forehead resting against the cool, worn wood siding as she stood beside me, her arms crossed, back stiff.

"Damn." I drew a steadying breath and turned back to face her. "All right. Something is up. But people I love are in some serious shit."

JT tilted her head toward me but remained silent, one eyebrow slightly arched in either curiosity or skepticism.

"I can't tell you—can't tell anyone, for that matter—until—until I take care of some … things." Lame. Too lame. I so badly wanted to tell her that evil men threatened to kill Eddy. I repressed the urge to shake her and tell her that my best friend had nothing to do with cold-blooded murder. I wobbled on the brink, wanted to scream at JT to fix it, to do her cop thing and make it all right. Instead, I said, "Really, JT, there's nothing you can do to help me right now."

She exhaled loudly and peered skyward, as if counting backward until she'd be calm enough to speak rationally. After a few agonizing moments, the shadows that were her eyes fastened on my face. "I could haul you downtown for questioning, you know."

The blood drained from my brain and for a minute, I thought I might drop right there.

JT must have sensed my panicked vibes and said slowly, "Jesus. Okay. Fine. Have it your way. For now. But, listen to me, Shay. Do you still have the card I gave you with my phone numbers on it?"

"Yeah."

JT gripped my shoulders and gave me a not-so-gentle shake. "Keep it with you. I want you to call me any time, day or night, if you're in trouble. Do you understand?"

"Why do you want to help me?"

"Because I'm a cop and that's what cops do." JT raised her hand and moved it toward my cheek again but stopped before she made contact. "Because my gut tells me you're okay. And I know you're in some deep crap that's going to bite you in the ass." Then she laughed. "And it doesn't hurt that I find you completely irresistible." She turned on her heel and walked away.

After a moment of stunned immobility, I shook myself like a dog and stumbled into the garage. The garage door rumbled shut, and I fled to the safety of the loft.

Coop was laughing so hard he was nearly doubled over. "I couldn't believe it when I come around the corner, and whoop, there she is!" Another guffaw burst out of him. "And then you glom onto her like a stray mutt with a hard-on for a rawhide. Oh my god!"

I held my head in my hands and replayed the entire episode in the theater of my mind.

Coop eventually dragged himself to the table and collapsed in a chair. "Okay, I think I'm under control. What was she doing here? What happened at Rita's?"

"One thing at a time. I don't know why JT was here. Besides spying on us. Guess Kate said something to her about things being a little 'off.'" I floated quotation marks in the air with my fingers. "So she decided to hang around. Seems like snooping to me."

"If she had more information, you think she'd have dragged you down to the station for some one-on-one, if you know what I mean." Coop had crass down to a science.

"She threatened. And stop smirking. You're damn lucky I did what I did or you'd be the one bending over and coughing for the cops. The least you could do is show me some appreciation."

We settled down, and I recounted my adventure with Rita and her mole. I also added my thoughts about the fact that perhaps Kinky really hadn't known where the truckload of nuts had gone, and maybe Rita and hubby were mired in this mess.

Once I finished, Coop leaned forward in his chair and banged his forehead against the tabletop. Alarmed, I made a grab to stop him and missed. "What *are* you doing?"

He thunked his head again and mumbled, "Sometimes it makes me think better."

This time I got a handful of hair. "You're insane. You'll scramble the only brains you have left if you do that again."

"Might help," he said, defeat echoing in his voice. "What now?"

"We need to get into that place on Washington and see if we can find something that'll tell us where the nuts went. A bill of lading, a transfer order ..."

Coop rubbed his hands together, his momentary tangle with doom giving way to a glimmer of hope. "We'll need some equipment. We're getting to be old hands at burgling."

Great. The last thing I wanted to become was an old hand at breaking and entering. But I didn't really have a choice. As darkness fell, we gathered up the paraphernalia Coop decided we needed and headed toward Lazar and Company Dry Storage.

Washington Avenue runs a fairly straight line from northeast Minneapolis through downtown and extends past 35W until it hooks a corner and drifts into the West Bank of the U of M. It cut through the Warehouse District, and in its day had been home to a number of strip clubs, biker bars, triple-X stores, and other questionable enterprises. In the last few years, the city council had worked to clean up the notorious avenue and forced a number of seedy sin, skin, and sex shops to close up. Apparently they missed one shady place.

We spotted the Lazar place and drove slowly past it. The red-brick building was half a city block long. The front butted up against the curb on Washington. I rounded the block and cruised past the parking lot, which was on the other side of the structure, out of view of the street. The LAZAR AND COMPANY DRY STORAGE sign, attached to a slightly bent metal post, was shiny new. The far corner of the lot was bathed in a pale glow from a streetlight, but the circle of light left most of the lot in darkness.

My headlights swept the area. The space was large enough to allow semi-trucks to turn around and back up to one of two loading docks. In addition, three other gigantic garage doors took up most of the rear of the building. At one end was an employee entrance lit from above by a bare bulb.

No cars occupied the lot, and the windows in the brick building were dark. No one was home. I pulled into an empty area adjacent to the warehouse and parked behind a dumpster. "Ready?" I asked.

"As I'll ever be."

We piled out of the truck dragging our implements of crime. Coop had a tire iron, some rope, a couple of screwdrivers, a flashlight, and a flat piece of metal he thought might pop locks open. Before you knew it, he'd be changing his name to MacGyver. Or we were both going to wind up as some prison daddy's bitches.

I had assorted screwdrivers, an old hammer, a flashlight, a pocket knife of my dad's, a pad of paper, two pens, and a playing-card-sized digital camera, all stuffed in various pockets of my sweatshirt and pants. Learning from our last illegal outing, we both wore work gloves instead of the hot and sweaty plastic kitchen ones we'd sported on the barge.

We slunk around the dumpster and made our way through the blackness toward the staff door. The air smelled musty, from the dumpster or the building, I didn't know. The asphalt was in worse shape than the crumbling building. "Coop—" I whispered loudly, "be careful—"

My warning came too late. There was an exhale of air, a clang of metal, and a muffled thud. I froze. Thankfully, I heard no more than the occasional sounds of vehicles on Washington Avenue as they whizzed past. No feet running to investigate, no sirens.

After a second that felt like ten, I whispered, "Coop, you okay?" I could make out his long form still sprawled on the ground.

"Yeah, except for a bit of missing skin. Rita should spend some dough fixing this place up instead of blowing it all on bingo. Where's the damn crow bar?" After some scuffing around, he stood. We forged on, creeping more cautiously across the treacherous terrain, and stopped outside of the puddle of light cast from a bare bulb above the door.

I said quietly, "Hope you can get it open. What if it's alarmed?"

"We'll never know till we try. If an alarm goes off, run."

"How long do you think it would be before the cops would show?"

"No idea."

"Oh God," I whispered. The hair was standing on end all over my body, and my heart was a few beats below stroke-out level.

Sucking in a breath, Coop held it, and then blew it out. "Wish me luck." He stepped up to the door. It looked like he was on a stage with a giant spotlight shining directly down on him. It's amazing how fear distorts reality.

Coop slid the thin strip of metal between the jamb and the door, wiggling it up and down. He worked at it for what felt like minutes until the door clicked, then swung open under the pressure of his fingertips. I peered into the black hole in surprise. Neither one of us thought he'd actually be able to jimmy it. We waited for the screech of an alarm. Nothing. Blessed silence reigned. Unless, of course, that blessed silence was a silent alarm that came to the attention of some security company or the fuzz.

We had no way of knowing. I dashed through the outer pool of light after Coop. He quietly shut the door, throwing us into almost total invisibility. We stood very still, ears on high alert. The periodic drone of a passing car outside was muted by the thick walls. The only other sound was our labored breathing.

"I think we made it," I said, voice low.

"Yeah." Coop flicked on his flashlight.

The open space felt endless and hollow, easily the size of three basketball courts. Six narrow windows, high above our heads, allowed faint light to seep in, but the slight illumination was quickly swallowed up by the interior darkness. The odor of old grease and dust was overpowering and the air tickled my nostrils, threatening to make me sneeze. To our left, Coop's light caught two doors on the far side of the raised loading dock.

"Come on," I said, pretending to possess the steely resolve brave people supposedly possessed in ample supply. The only thing I possessed at the moment was still-clean underwear, but I wasn't sure how long that was going to last. I aimed for a set of stairs that led to the top of the loading dock.

My flashlight revealed cracked and stained concrete. Sand, pebbles, leaves, and twigs littered the floor, probably blown inside when the huge garage doors were rolled up to receive or send out shipments. Our footsteps were silent with the exception of the occasional crunch of a brittle leaf.

We moved cautiously up the stairs. The top of the loading dock was vast and bare. I shone my light on the two doors.

I whispered, "Game show contestant, do you select door number one or door number two?"

"Door number two, please."

The doorknob twisted easily in my hand. I held my breath and eased it open. Inside, the darkness was so complete that my flashlight barely cut a swath. My nose, however, informed me we were in a very smelly john.

I fumbled against the wall for a light switch. My fingers caught it, and I waited for Coop to step inside behind me. "Shut the door and I'll turn on the light."

The door clicked shut, and I flipped the switch. We stood in the can, squinting as our eyes adjusted. I hoped the prevalence of bathrooms in our investigations was not a harbinger that our efforts were about to go down the toilet. A porcelain sink, perilously attached to the wall, sported old-fashioned, gunk-covered spigots for hot and cold. The basin was stained a rusty color beneath each faucet, and in the silence I heard a plink as water leaked from one or maybe both fixtures. The ring in the toilet bowl was the same dirty brown, and the seat was a curious baby blue. Ugh.

"Unless you have to go, I think we can skip this room," Coop said.

"Yeah—no thanks."

Coop shut off the light and we backed out.

Door number one was also unlocked. As it swung open, a stench I had no idea how to identify slammed into us with the force of a Mack truck. I flipped the switch, shedding light on a dreary office furnished with an old wooden desk, three battered filing cabinets, and one very dead body reclining in a chair behind said desk.

Coop whispered, "Oh shit."

The man had been shot smack-dab between his eyes, the point of entry making a neat part in the unibrow that ran from one side of his forehead to the other. His head was tilted back, arms hanging limply over the armrests. He was dressed in a turtleneck sweater and leather bomber jacket. The wall behind him was speckled with something ghastly, and the metallic scent of blood and other vileness filled the room.

Behind me, Coop gagged and ran. I wondered if I'd be next. Forcing a swallow, I tried to breathe through my mouth. Was this Mr. Luther Lazar? My feet were rooted to the spot, and I had to work to keep myself from swaying. Air in mouth, out nose. Do not throw up. I hated throwing up.

The toilet flushed noisily next door, and the sound of running water seeped into the roar of horror that rung in my ears. In another minute, Coop was next to me, his jaws vigorously working a stick of gum. "Sorry about that. I'm okay now. Here, it'll help." He handed me a piece of Juicy Fruit. I hoped it would chase the taste of death from my mouth. We both chomped loudly.

"We have to call the cops," I eventually said.

We chewed some more.

Coop shook his head. "This might be our only chance to find the nuts."

More gum gnashing. If my brain had been functioning, I'd have been amazed at Coop's sudden composure. He said, "Let's see what we can find, and we'll be really careful not to mess up any evidence."

My jaw was getting sore. "Okay. So. We'll call the police once we're safely out of here, unlike—Dead Dude."

Coop squinted at the body, head tilted as if he were studying a piece of artwork. "I think it's a guy that's come to the Bingo Barge with Rita a couple of times."

I tried to suppress a gag. The Juicy Fruit was becoming cloyingly sweet. "I think we should get out of here."

Coop didn't respond right away, and I knocked him with my elbow.

Tearing his gaze away from the body, Coop looked at me. His eyes reflected revulsion and curiosity. His eyebrows floated at his hairline. "Dead Dude's not going to do anything. We've got to figure out what happened to the truckload of almonds. Big picture and all that. Remember it's about Eddy, Shay ..." He trailed off, his hand slowly dropping to his side, his eyes drawn irresistibly back to the corpse.

I fought harder against the urge to hurl. "I know. You're right." Still, neither of us moved. "You ever see a dead body before?" I asked, hands pressed hard to my midsection.

"Only in a funeral home."

I forced one foot in front of another and crept closer to Dead Dude, until I stood directly in front of the desk, breathing hard out of my mouth. The workspace was cluttered with bills of lading, scribbled notes on torn paper, an open ledger, and a paper coffee cup, contents spilled onto the top of everything. I edged around the corner of the desk, my head pounding. On the floor below Dead Dude's left hand lay a palm-sized black revolver.

I carefully sucked some air. "Coop, come here."

Coop took a tentative step toward me, then two. Then he was next to me, his face fixed in a horrified grimace. "You think he offed himself?"

I attempted to compartmentalize my fear and study the body as if I were in an anatomical forensics class. One eye was open and the other was closed. How was that possible? I winked my own eye shut, then shuddered. The open eye was blue-gray. Freaky. How in the world did I get stuck standing in front of a dead man? I was a simple coffee shop co-owner who steered clear of the law, didn't bother anyone, and was, for the most part, a decent human being.

I stifled a groan. "He could have killed himself, I suppose." I eyed the cadaver. "But Coop, do you think you could hold a gun and shoot yourself right between the eyes?"

Coop formed his hand into a gun and pointed it at the center of his forehead. But where would the gun land after the trigger was pulled? I didn't think it would wind up on the floor right below the corpse's dangling hand. That hand would probably land in his lap. I ran that thought out loud as I fought against a wave of nausea. That would really taint the crime scene.

"Makes sense. Someone comes in while Dead Dude—who's not yet dead—is working, shoots him, and then drops the gun there to make it look like a suicide. You want to find his wallet and see who he is?"

Coop blanched at my suggestion. "Shay, we can't mess up evidence. And no way am I touching him."

I sighed. Bile bubbled in my throat, making my Juicy Fruit bitter. "This is an emergency situation. I won't touch anything but his wallet. You check on his desk." I closed my eyes for a moment, trying to stop the room from swaying. I could not believe I was about to search a *dead* guy. Oh, no, actually, a *murdered* dead guy. Oh God.

Coop put the desk between the dead man and himself. I gingerly reached out and lifted the zippered edge of his leather jacket. Nothing. I moaned. Tried the other side of the jacket, hoping I wouldn't have to check his pants pockets. This time I felt a weight within and carefully extracted a wallet from an inner pocket, being very careful not to touch anything else.

"Got it," I said, and flipped it open. The license was right on top, in a clear plastic sleeve. "It is Luther Lazar. Wonder if Miss Personality knows hubby is dead?" I held the license up to compare the dead guy to the photo. The man on it didn't look much more alive than the corpse in the chair. It was an undeniable match. I gingerly replaced the wallet. My hand inadvertently brushed against Luther's cold shirt front, and I shuddered.

Backing away rapidly, I pivoted and headed for the filing cabinets. I stood still, my eyes closed, willing my innards to calm. Then I opened the top drawer of one of the tan-colored cabinets. It was empty. "Huh," I said. "The whole cabinet is empty. Not a scrap of paper, not a single file."

"What about the others?"

I stepped sideways and tugged on the top drawer. Empty. The next one yielded a couple of stacks of blank invoices, some pads of note paper, and other assorted office supplies. "Rita did say they'd been getting ready to move. Maybe they cleared everything out already."

"Maybe," Coop said, clearly distracted. He was carefully sifting though the piles on the desktop.

I pulled the bottom drawer on the last cabinet open. A few files were jammed in the very back of the drawer. I wondered if they'd been left intentionally or simply missed. The folders held various bills. I paged through them, realizing that every one of them was overdue.

"Hey, Coop, check this out. They're behind on …" I flipped a page. "The utility bill—damn, get this, by over two grand." More flipping. "And electric. It's huge—almost five thousand dollars." I skimmed through bill after bill. "The garbage company, property taxes. You name it. They haven't paid anything for months."

I flashed back to Rita's house and the lack of furniture. Maybe it hadn't all been packed away in preparation for a move but had been sold instead. "Coop, what kind of a gambler was Rita?"

Coop paused in his paperwork perusal. "What do you mean?"

"Was she a high roller, or a conservative spender? Did she cough up a lot of money when she came in to play?"

He blew air out between pursed lips. "She always spent seventy-five or a hundred bucks on bingo every session she was there, but that was beans compared to the amount of money she threw at pulltabs. A couple thousand a crack wasn't unusual."

"And how often did she play?"

"I'd say she was in maybe five or six times a week."

I did some fast calculations in my head. "She was probably dropping somewhere in the area of ten grand a week. Even with the occasional win, she had to be leaking money like a sieve."

"Yeah. Something to think about." He returned his attention to the papers in his hands. I stood up, pressing my fists against my now-aching lower back. I took a step toward the desk to help Coop, and then backtracked and retrieved the overdue bills, spread them on the floor, and took a photograph of each. I carefully replaced the bills in the folders and the folders in the cabinet. Gotta love digital cameras.

Coop finished going through the loose papers. I carefully pulled the ledger off the desktop and tilted it to drain off the spilled coffee. I watched the familiar sight of coffee drops splattering on a floor, and my brain squeezed tight within my skull. We had to be in some kind of alternate universe. Everything was completely unreal. We were making a guest appearance in the middle of someone else's night terrors. Or we were stoned on 'shrooms and having a horrible trip. I clenched my teeth and turned my attention to the ledger.

Each entry included a concise list of shipments coming in, what was going out, storage charges, and additional fees. The initial entry at the front of the book was dated three years prior. I paged through to the end, and the last line was filled in the day before yesterday for a Con-Rail shipment consisting of two containers that were bound for Pennsylvania.

I flipped the beige pages with their precise blue lines to the date the nuts should have arrived, the 17th. Four entries were neatly printed in a row. The first was the arrival of a Priority Express truck dropping off three pallets of something for some company I'd never heard of. The second entry was the departure of three containers headed for the Minneapolis Railway Loading Facility.

The third entry in the log was the arrival of a truck with an unidentified load, slated to be stored until Monday, November 22nd, the same date from the business card from Kinky's office. That had to be it! The fourth logged shipment was the arrival of two pallets for F&D Linen.

I was about to tell Coop what I found when he yelped, and I just about shot out of my shoes.

"Shay—I've got it!" He waved a sheet of paper at me. I stuck a finger in the ledger to keep my place as I walked over to him.

"This is a bill of lading for the transfer of a truck loaded with perishable dry goods to," he squinted at the cramped printing. "Brooklyn Park. There's no business name, only an address: 7765 Wyland Avenue."

"What's the date?"

"Friday—the nineteenth."

I gently set the ledger on the edge of the desk and tried to ignore Lazar's one-eyed stare as I opened it. "Coop, it fits. Is there some kind of a logging, or tracking number…" I trailed off as I scanned the suspect ledger entry from the 17th. "1274—"

"682," Coop finished. Our gaze's locked. We'd found where the truck was taken. Now we could only hope it was still there.

TEN

WE DIGITALLY DOCUMENTED OUR finds and gave Luther our last respects. After a brief argument about who would call the cops and tell them a very dead man waited patiently for the undertaker, I gave in and called 911 anonymously from one of the few remaining payphones on the planet. The criminal counts against us were steadily rising.

Once we were back on the road, Coop said, "Poor Luther. I know we had to leave him, but he's sitting there all stiff and alone in the cold. I feel terrible saying this, but I'm actually starving. And I need a smoke so bad I could cry."

My barely tamped-down guilt rose again like thick fog. We'd broken into another business. We'd fled the scene of another crime we'd messed with. We were felons. With great effort, I poked the fog of guilt back into its proverbial bottle and stuck a figurative cork in it. There'd be time for self-flagellation later. I opened my mouth, shut it, and then said, "Coop. We didn't kill him. We happened to find him. We did him a favor by calling the police. As for your other two issues, I can help you out with one of those requests."

Coop vetoed my vote for McDonalds on moral grounds. I found a Subway and pulled in. While I ordered a veggie sub for Coop and a ham and cheese on honey-wheat for me, he dallied outside, feeding his nicotine addiction. As I paid the way-too-young-to-be-working, acne-faced Sandwich Artist for our subs, Coop came inside. His face was bright red, probably from sucking so hard on his cigarette.

We snarfed our sandwiches in record time, and Coop ordered another to go for later. I never understood how he managed to pack away the food he ate and still remain as thin as he did. Must be the vegetarian thing.

"Tell me the address again," I said to Coop. We exited off 94 to 694 and headed north to Brooklyn Park.

"7765 Wyland Avenue."

Neither of us was familiar with the area, so I pulled off the highway and into a Wendy's parking lot and hauled out my Hudson's map book. After some discussion, we were back on the road.

The place was located in a northern suburb of Minneapolis. The area transitioned from residential housing to industrial, with many businesses behind chainlink fences. I tried to help Coop watch for building numbers, which were always hard to find, and doubly so when it was dark. I was about to give up when we spotted a two-story building set back from the road, its roof peaking above a weathered, wooden privacy fence. Isolated, with no close neighbors on either side, the gate bore a rusting sign with the number 7765. Nothing identified the business within.

"Where do you think I should park?" I asked.

"We just passed a parking lot that wrapped behind the building. Head back there."

I flipped a U-turn and slowly passed 7765 Wyland again. A grove of trees stood between it and the parking lot we were headed for about a half mile away. I was happy to see the micro forest, thinking it would give us a bit of cover.

On foot, we dodged through the trees to the long fence bordering the property. At this point I felt a little like Robin Hood, stealing from the rich for the benefit of the poor—or in our case for the benefit of Eddy's life. The tree line stopped twenty feet from the fence. I panted from attempting to keep up with Coop's long legs and had given up badgering him to slow down for me. Chalk up another one for the vegetarians, I guess.

We checked the gate, and after finding it locked tight, headed around the corner of the wood-plank fence, away from the road.

The fence was a good three feet over Coop's head. "Boost me up, and I'll hop over," I told him. "If the coast is clear, you can climb over after me." Coop cupped his hands and heaved me skyward. My fingers caught the top of the barrier, and I was glad it was solid wood and not barbed wire. With some effort I hauled myself to the top and scoped the grounds.

Cars in various states of disrepair lined the enclosure of a massive junkyard. Thanks to the metal corpses, my drop would be cut by almost half. I swung one leg over, and then the other, hanging by my arms as the aroma of old junkers tickled my nostrils. The smell reminded me of a car my parents had when I was a kid, an old Ford Falcon many years past its prime. I paused, surprised at the visceral recollection from before I even knew how to tie my own shoes.

Coop gave me the thumbs up and flashed me a lopsided, encouraging smile. I landed on the roof of the car below me with a soft thud. My feet dented the roof ever so slightly as I wobbled, caught my balance, and then held as still as I could, my senses on high alert. One unlit light post leaned at a cockeyed angle in the front of a long, corrugated metal building at the center of the junkyard.

The building was long and narrow. Two garage doors on the far end of the structure probably led into automotive bays of some kind. Three beat-up demolition derby cars, numbers painted on their dented sides, were parked in front of the building. The building's windows were black, and I hoped that meant the place was devoid of human life.

I was about to hop to the ground when I heard the faint sound of metal clinking. My already-galloping heart shifted into high gear. The sound definitely wasn't the wind. The jingle stopped, and then almost before I could blink, a gargantuan hound dog came loping across the compound straight toward me.

Dogs don't usually scare me, but this one was the size of a miniature horse, with the head of a Boxer and the body of bulldozer. Its cheeks jounced up and down as it bounded toward me. The owner of the mutt had clipped its tail but left its ears uncropped, and they bounced in tandem with the flapping lips.

I froze on the roof of the car, automobile-surfing, my arms outstretched. "Nice doggy," I whispered. "Nice doggy."

The dog came to a screeching halt directly below me, eyes never leaving my face. I expected voluminous barking to pierce the air. "COOP," I tried to yell in a whisper.

Coop's voice filtered over the fence, "What's up?"

"DOG!"

"What? I can't hear you."

I tried again, louder this time, in a low voice instead of a whisper. "BIG DOG!"

"Hang on. The sub … I'll throw it over."

"Coop," I hissed, "dogs aren't vegetarians!"

"Don't worry, dogs aren't picky. Here it comes."

I dragged my eyes from the huge pooch in time to see the ghostly apparition of a Subway sandwich sailing over the fence. I managed to dart a hand out and grab the plastic bag before it hit the car roof and bounced to the hard-packed dirt below. My eyes returned to the dog, who now sat on gigantic haunches, the floppy lip on one side of its mouth hooked on a bottom tooth, head tilted curiously at me. I couldn't tell if the fang was bared in a growl I couldn't hear, or if the dog's loose lip was simply snagged on it.

"Good puppy," I said hopefully. I slowly crouched low on the roof of the car, my eyes never leaving the dog, which observed everything I did but didn't move. In fact, the animal still hadn't uttered a peep. I slowly opened the plastic and with trembling fingers ripped at the paper around the sub. Thank God Coop wasn't vegan, or there'd be no cheese to tempt the mutt with. Even if Coop figured the dog would chow down on whatever I offered, I wasn't too sure it would like jalapeños, pickles, and olives.

I pulled off a healthy hunk of bread and withdrew it from the bag. The dog hadn't budged, it simply sat there waiting. "Good dog," I said to it again, and tossed the bread. The mutt leaped into the air in a burst of coiled muscle, nabbed the bread, and landed gracefully. It rolled over onto its back, and waved its paws at me. From that position I ascertained that it was actually a he.

Geez, the only thing scary about this dog was his size. I tossed him another chunk of bread, which he scrambled up to get. He returned and sat in front of me again, lower tooth hanging out, and softly whined. I gingerly slid off the car. The animal made no move toward me. He sat there waiting, his butt shaking as he wagged his invisible tail.

Bending down again, I extended my hand with another hunk of the sandwich. "Easy boy," I whispered, and moved close enough so he could take the food from my fingers. He delicately accepted it, his eyes glued to me as he appeared to roll the bread around his mouth before swallowing it. Then he bent his head and something hit the hard-packed dirt. At first I thought he was going to throw up, and then I flashed the light at his head. He'd spit out a pickle. He raised his big head and gazed at me with pleading eyes.

"Coop," I called out in a low voice.

"Yeah, you okay?"

"Fine. This dog is not a fan of pickles." I proceeded to rip the rest of the sandwich into bite-size pieces and set them on the ground. The mutt leaned his great big head over the offering. I reached out and stroked his ears, and then slid my hand up his warm, soft neck. When I reached his back I felt the bones of his spine. This pooch wasn't getting nearly enough to eat. I ran my hands down his sides and over ribs that jutted through taut skin.

When he'd finished the sandwich chunks, the dog sat again, and I laughed aloud when I saw a mound of green on the ground. I peered closer. It was all pickles, not a single jalapeño in the pile.

I stood up, and the dog shifted his butt over to lean against me. His bones pressed against my leg right through my pants. He gazed up at me with big Boxer eyes and whined softly. He was clearly neglected and starved for food and attention. It infuriated me when people abused animals that couldn't fight back. I put my hand on the top of his broad head and he pushed against me.

Suddenly both of us were startled by a loud thunk on the fence. The dog yipped and ducked behind me at the sound and movement, but not before I saw the whites of his eyes almost glowing in the dark. Coop seemed to sail over the top of the fence like a pole vaulter gone mad. His long legs gave him so much momentum that he skimmed the top of the car I'd landed on and crashed onto the ground in a heap. He didn't move and didn't utter a sound. For a moment, I was afraid he'd killed himself.

Before I made a move toward him, the dog slunk around me and warily scooted on stiff legs toward my fallen comrade. I reached out to restrain the animal, but he was too fast. He straddled Coop and let loose with his big tongue, slurping Coop's face from chin to forehead. That was enough to rouse Coop from his lack-of-air stupor. He flailed his arms wildly, choking. "Get this thing off me! He's killing me!" I dragged the dog off so Coop could sit up, swearing and spitting and wiping away slobber.

As Coop tried to catch his breath, I felt around the pooch's leather collar. A name tag hung on a metal loop. In the beam of my flashlight one side read Dawg. The other side was imprinted with the name Buzz Riley, and this Brooklyn Park address.

"Coop," I said, "I think this is Buzz Riley's place."

"What?"

"Yeah, that's the name on the dog's tag. And who would name a dog Dawg? D-A-W-G. That's plain wrong. And Buzz is starving and probably beating this dog too." Dawg wagged his butt and pushed himself against my leg again.

"Riley's a real ass. He gets into arguments with the Bingo Barge staff and the customers. Rumor has it he ran someone over on purpose during one of those hick county fair shows where they bash each other's cars apart trying to knock them out of the competition."

"I think you mean a demolition derby."

"Whatever. He's big and mean. Doesn't surprise me he'd name a dog Dawg and not take care of him." Coop made it to his feet and dusted himself off. "Okay, let's take a poke around this joint and get out. I don't want to be here if Buzz decides to make an appearance."

We headed toward the building, our progress less difficult because the clouds cleared away and the stars and moon had appeared, giving us enough illumination to safely pick our way to the main door.

The door was unlocked and opened with a resounding screech. I ducked and Coop flattened himself against the outside wall. Even Dawg bounced back a couple of feet. Apparently Buzz felt secure enough with his fence and his bulky guard dog that he didn't think locking up his shop was necessary. When no threat presented itself, I tentatively stepped across the threshold.

The smell of oil, gas, and burned rubber permeated the room. I scanned the area with my flashlight. We were in what once had been some kind of show room that had deteriorated into an ungodly mess. Filthy car parts in various states of assembly rested on every available surface as well as on the concrete floor. Toward the rear of the room, double doors stood open into a black, cavernous space.

Once inside, Coop pulled the door shut and I shuddered at the reverse screech. I slowly made my way toward the deep blackness beyond the double doors with Coop and Dawg at my heels.

Even with both our flashlight beams, we couldn't see much of the dark interior. Cars were lined up with parts strewn on the ground around them, some of the bodies stripped and primed for painting. Many of them looked brand-new.

"Man," Coop said, "now I know how Buzz affords his gambling."

I carefully walked past the row of cars. "What do you mean?"

"This," Coop shone his light around, bouncing it off cars and parts, "is a chop shop."

We continued along the edge of the building. Déjà vu. The black interior felt so deep I thought it might never end. I stopped abruptly at a huge vehicle illuminated by our flashlights. A body ran into me because of my sudden stop, and it wasn't Coop's. Dawg ambled around me and plopped his big butt on my shoe again. I absently scratched the top of his head. Then it dawned on me the thing was a big rig, a tow truck on steroids, meant to haul semis and other gargantuan vehicles.

"That's a hell of a tow truck," Coop said.

We trudged around the behemoth, and my heart sank. An open area of concrete sported some recently dripped oil stains, and the space was large enough that it could have held a semi, but there was no truck with ALMONDS written on the side.

We shone our lights here and there, and Dawg decided to detach himself from my side and sniff the floor. I heard a distinct crunch. Dawg looked over his thick shoulder at me, his expression both happy and guilty, waiting to see if I was going to yell or not. When he decided he wasn't going to get hollered at, he put his nose back to the dirty floor. I heard him snort. His tongue slapped something, and then he made another crunch.

Coop shone his flashlight on Dawg, who wore the same delighted expression he'd had when I'd given him the sub outside.

"What's he eating?" Coop asked.

Seven or eight almonds were scattered on the floor around Dawg's sizeable paws. Dawg put his nose back to the floor and wheezed some more, devouring the nuts as if they were hors d'oeuvres. "Almonds! The truck had to be here at some point."

Coop played his light around the floor, but the rest of the area was absent of incriminating evidence. In another moment, the concrete was almond-free, thanks to our canine cleanup. We moved toward the rear of the building, and the beam from Coop's flashlight caught the reflection of a burned-out exit sign above a back door.

We continued our tour, returning to the front via the opposite side of the long row of disassembled cars. I was about to say we should probably get out of there when I was cut off by the screech of the front door, followed by voices that were loud but unintelligible. Bright lights flashed on in the front room, slicing into the darkness. Could déjà vu happen twice in the space of five minutes? This was so similar to the events on the barge the night before that I was beginning to believe we were stuck in a time warp, à la *Groundhog Day*.

We killed our flashlights and ducked behind one of the in-progress car remodels. My heart hammered in my ears. At least we didn't have to breathe in the stench from a rank men's room. We were about midway between the front and back of the long building, and I fleetingly wondered if we should keep going or backtrack and see if we could sneak out the exit door we'd glimpsed.

The voices grew louder, and Coop whispered, "Holy shit, it's Buzz!"

ELEVEN

"GODDAMN GOOD FOR NOTHING dog, off hidin' somewhere. Should be shot." We heard a gleeful guffaw and the sound of something hard slapping leather. Then Buzz's booming laughter echoed as he and another man exited the front room and entered the huge space.

The other man said, "Ow, that hurt! Take your aggravations out on the mutt. Rita's a rich bitch—too rich for trailer park trash like you."

"Artie, I told you once not to touch me. You touched me. And Rita ain't a bitch. She might be rich, she's definitely stupid, but she ain't a bitch."

"If she's not a bitch, why you so mad at her?"

"Because, asshole, she talked to that woman who came poking around about the warehouse. That was too close. The deal's damn near done. Those fucking nuts'll be on a boat headed down the Mississippi tomorrow night, and we'll all get paid. Then Rita and me's goin' south." A rasping, evil laugh sent a shiver down my spine. "Waaay fucking south."

The men's voices grew louder as they approached, and only the hulking remains of cars were between us now. I was afraid Dawg would bolt and run to Buzz, effectively announcing our presence.

I groped out a hand and as soon as I touched fur, the dog crowded close to me, quivering. In a fit of instantaneous, almost blind rage, I nearly jumped up and screamed at Buzz and his redneck pal. Coop must have sensed I was about to do something stupid. He grabbed my arm.

Buzz said in a raspy growl, "Fuck it. I'm going for the shotgun. See if Dawg's on top of his game tonight or not."

Dawg cowered even lower. The two men headed back the way they'd come, their voices fading in time to their steps.

"We have to get out," Coop whispered. "The door back there. Maybe we can sneak out and they'll never know we were here."

We crept toward the rear corner of the building. My foot caught on some mechanical part, and I stumbled, going down on one knee. Dawg immediately came to my aid, slurping the back of my head. Coop nudged the heavy pooch away and hauled me to my feet, trying to keep his profile low in case Buzz and Artie returned. I brushed my hands on the seat of my pants and scrambled after him. We made it to the door without further incident, and Coop turned the knob. He pushed it open just enough to see if the coast was clear.

Harsh voices echoed across the big compound.

"DAWG!"

"Here, you mangy mutt!"

"I can't believe that damn animal. Some watchdog he is!"

Coop stuck his head out, and then ducked back in. "Junkers are lined up right next to the fence back here, too. I say we make a break for it, hop onto that old red car and then over the fence."

Dawg sat between us, his massive head pivoting from Coop to me and back to Coop, as if he were following the conversation. I patted his neck and put my cheek against his floppy ear. "You come with me, boy. But if you can't, I swear we'll come back and get you out of this crap hole." I hoped Dawg could follow instructions and had good leaping abilities.

"Ready?" Coop asked.

"Yeah. On three, let's go."

The voices came closer, yelling out various Dawg insults, comparing him to portions of the female anatomy. "Coop—" I began, intending to say that maybe we should wait until Buzz and Artie backed off a distance. But Coop made the break and streaked toward the fence.

I swore under my breath. It was now or never. If they spotted Coop, it was all over. With a shout of, "Dawg! Come!" I burst out of the door and charged after him, hands fisted, arms pumping.

Coop's feet hit the trunk of a rusty old Ford Taurus with a metallic crunch, and he leaped for the roof. I was about ten yards behind him when I heard the unmistakable ratchet of the slide slamming home a shotgun shell.

"Artie, what— hey, STOP! That's the bingo freak—can't miss that fuckin' scarecrow. And someone's with him!"

Shouts echoed as I surged onto the trunk. Coop slithered over the top of the fence and disappeared.

I jumped onto the roof of the car and took a flying leap, reaching for the top of the fence. The rough wood bit into my fingers. I struggled to swing my leg over the edge. A blast roared in my head. The wood next to my right arm splintered, shards flying everywhere.

If ever I wished to be taller, the time was now. I managed to hook one foot over the fence, almost home free.

The sound of toenails scraping against rusting paint pierced my haze of desperation. I glanced to my right and saw Dawg had scrambled to the roof of the car next to me and was about to launch himself toward the top of the wood barrier. God, please let him make it over the top.

"Damn, can't believe ya missed that target. Hey Buzz! There's your freakin' dog—shoot him!" The hammering bark of the shotgun shattered the night again. I flinched, waiting for Dawg's yelp of pain.

With a great heave, I shouted, "DAWG! Jump!" and surged up and over the edge. I heard another rack of the shotgun. The belch of the weapon and impact of the shot against the fence was instantaneous. I tried to get my feet under me, but the ground came faster than I could react.

I hit the earth hard and landed in a heap like a rag doll, my eyes wide as I tried to breathe.

I rolled to my back and watched stars twinkling overhead. I thought I saw the Big Dipper as I fought for air. I was interrupted from my stargazing by the largest falling star I'd ever seen sailing over me. I blinked. It took on the shape of a dog, and I decided I was hallucinating, watching Dawg go to animal heaven. I even heard the jingle of his collar one last time, followed by a loud thud.

More shouting came from the other side of the wood fence, and heavy boots banged on the hollow metal of a trashed car. Buzz yelled, "Boost me up, Artie. I'll take another shot. Assholes are kidnapping my damn dog!" The ratchet of the shotgun sounded far too close for comfort.

Suddenly something wet nuzzled my ear, and then Dawg really was there. I was never so happy to be drooled on. Coop frantically dragged me to my feet. I wrapped an arm around him and we hobbled through the trees as fast as we could. He was limping, and my right shoulder hurt like the dickens. One side of my face was wet with dog slobber, and my right arm stung in multiple spots. Dawg trotted along next to us, head high, as if he were proud as hell that he wasn't ever going back.

After what seemed like an eternity of scurrying along inside the wood line, out of sight of the road, we made it to my truck. I wondered if the gunshots attracted enough attention that someone would call the police.

We crammed ourselves in the cab, Dawg tucked firmly between Coop and me. His big nose almost hit the windshield. Oh Lord. Now we could add dog-napping to our growing list of crimes.

The clock on the dash glowed 10:03 and we still had no idea where the nuts were. I prayed Eddy was unhurt and giving her kidnapper one hell of a hard time as I stomped on the accelerator, intent on putting as many miles as I could between us and the lunatic with the gun.

———

Coop punched the remote when I pulled up to the garage. The door rumbled down behind us even before I'd shut the motor off.

Coop and I looked over Dawg's head at each other, half amazed we'd survived another crazy B&E adventure.

Dawg sat very still, his tongue lolling out one side of his mouth. "I think we've got a bit more on our hands than expected," I said.

"No shit." Coop gently tugged on Dawg's ear and was slurped. "Come on. Let's assess the damage."

We clamored out of the truck, and I tied a length of rope to Dawg's collar and walked him outside the garage. I patted him down and was relieved to not find any shotgun damage. The poor mutt's mental state had to be a whole different story.

I could hardly believe what had transpired in the last twenty-four hours. If the skies opened up and it rained dollar bills from heaven, I wouldn't be surprised.

Dawg did his business—his very *large* business—and we slipped back inside the garage. Coop had the loft trap door open and was in the process of tying rope to an old blue saucer sled.

"What are you doing?"

Coop tugged a knot tight. "Can't leave Dawg down here by himself."

"You plan on dragging him up there?"

"Damn straight. He's been through enough. He needs us." As if to punctuate that point, Dawg gazed at me with soulful eyes, his lip again caught on his bottom tooth.

For the next ten minutes we worked, tying a rope here, adding a pulley there, and Coop deemed the Dawg Hauler ready. It was a good effort, but I didn't think the giant pooch would sit still in the sled and allow us to pull him to the ceiling. I stood on the floor with Dawg while Coop crawled up into the loft.

Coop hollered, "Okay."

Dawg stared balefully at me. "Okay pal, let's see what happens." It took very little coaxing to get Dawg into the sled. He sat on his haunches and woofed softly at me. I smoothed his silky ears. "You stay, don't move. You'll be fine." Dawg's tongue slapped at my face. "Okay, go," I called out.

Inch by inch the sled rose. I fully expected Dawg to hop out with every tug. Instead he sat as still as could be, his eyes glued to mine. At last his head popped though the trap door, and in another second the sled bumped the ceiling. Dog nails scraped plastic as he scrambled out of the sled, and then Coop pulled it into the loft.

"I'll be damned," I whispered.

Coop called down, "Want a ride?"

"No, thank you. I prefer the ladder."

"Good," he replied as I climbed up. "That dog was heavy enough."

Dawg sniffed as he wandered around, taking in his new surroundings. He padded to the couch, sniffed some more, and then meandered to the bed. Without preamble, as if he'd done it a million times, he lumbered up on the mattress, circled around a couple of times, and plopped down with a heavy sigh.

Coop put a bowl of fresh water on the floor for Dawg while I rummaged around the small refrigerator, pulled out some deli-sliced ham, and piled the contents of the entire container on a plate. As soon as the fridge opened, Dawg hopped off the bed and ambled over to me. I set the plate down, and in no more than two and a half seconds, his tongue swiped up the last bit of ham. He looked up at me, then back at the empty plate.

I stared down at the top of Dawg's head and said, "Sorry, bud. No more." Dawg padded back to the bed, bounced up, and settled in again, resting his head on his paws. "Man, that puts a new spin on inhaling your food."

"No doubt," Coop said as he wet a paper towel in the tiny sink. He'd shed his jeans and stood in very manly bright-yellow Spongebob Squarepants boxers. He gingerly dabbed at a two-inch gash in his knee.

I pulled my sweatshirt off. The stinging I'd felt earlier on my arm was fence splinters from the shotgun blast. I pulled out three needle-like shards of wood from my skin, and more from the cloth of my shirt. If Buzz's aim had been any better, half of me would still be at the junkyard.

Both Coop and I had numerous cuts and scrapes, but nothing that wouldn't heal. We slapped on some Band-Aids I found. I swiveled my shoulder around, and it felt stiff but operable. Once patched up, we collapsed into chairs at the table.

Coop slouched with a hand under his chin, looking every bit as pooped as I felt. He said, "God, I really thought we'd found the nuts this time."

"Me too. We've been shot down twice. Literally. But we need to get our heads back in the game. Let's make a list of what we've found and figure out what to do next."

"We have one very dead Luther Lazar." Coop paused, and then groaned. "We're going to go straight to the furnace for ditching him."

"I thought you didn't believe in hell."

"Now's not the time to get technical." He was probably right. After all we'd done this night, we probably had first-class tickets. "So, where were we?"

"Luther's dead," I said. "And it sounds like Buzz is having a fling with Rita. Did Rita have Buzz whack Luther for her? Or is Lazar an unfortunate victim of our friendly Mafiosos?"

"I vote for Buzz. He's the kind of guy you might turn to if you needed someone dispatched into the great beyond."

"You think Rita is planning on taking off for points south with our buddy Buzz, or is she ditching him, too?"

Coop pondered that for a moment. "It sounds like he's up to his short hairs in the nuts deal. He thinks he's going with her."

I shuddered. "What on earth would a woman—who for all intents and purposes is on the moneyed end of the social spectrum—see in Redneck Riley?"

"It's all about sex, drugs, and rock 'n' roll, babe," Coop said with a grin. "Maybe he's got the right equipment."

I shot him a that's-way-too-gross-to-imagine look. "Maybe he's her hired hand, and she's stringing him along."

"I'm sorry to interrupt the regularly scheduled programming, but where are we going to search for the nuts now? We've got just over twelve hours before our delivery deadline."

We stared blankly at each other. Dawg shifted on the bed, and a momentary hissing noise emanated from the environs of his rear end.

"Coop, did that dog just fart?"

"I think—" Before he got out another word the odor hit us, and my eyes watered. I fanned the air. "Holy cow, we are *not* feeding that mutt any more Subway sandwiches or ham."

"Agreed," said Coop, a hand covering his nose. He got up and opened the trap door. Fat lot of good it did.

"Okay," I said, trying to breath through my mouth. "We know the nuts are supposed to be shipped down the Mississippi tomorrow, sometime in the evening. Where on the river do barges load these days? Dad hasn't worked on the river for years."

"No clue." He pulled the laptop open and started punching keys. After ten minutes, Coop shook his head. "There's twenty different shipping terminals on the Mississippi in the Twin Cities area. How do we figure out which one has the nuts?"

I drummed my fingers on the tabletop. "What if you narrow the terminal locations by what they ship? Terminal setups that ship edible goods have to be able to handle liquid and dry product. My dad once said some won't take that kind of stuff at all."

"Okay." Coop's fingers tapped the keyboard rapidly. "I'll do a search excluding recycling barges, automotive shipping, and terminals dedicated to specific companies, like 3M."

He waited for the page to load and said, "Let's see, it narrows the field down to three. Ribau Containers Inc. deals mostly with sugar, sand, iron ore … All dry goods. Packer Industries exports liquid and dry goods. The last one is the Grizzly Terminal & Dock Company."

I said, "I think it's time to make a quick trip to see a man about a bear."

TWELVE

My father, Pete O'Hanlon, was third generation Irish/American. His granddad arrived at Ellis Island in the late 1800s and settled in New York until a brother talked him into moving to Minnesota, a land ripe with opportunity for hard-working men.

The Korean Conflict was in full swing when my dad hit seventeen, and he lied about his age in order to follow his best friend into the Navy. I'd always had a sneaking suspicion that his patriotism was an attempt to avoid the rampant alcoholism passed down from generation to generation, all the way from Ireland. As it turned out, my father couldn't run far enough or fast enough to escape his genes, and the bottle found him anyway. He was honorably discharged with a purple heart, a bum knee, and an unquenchable thirst for firewater.

Often my father didn't appear inebriated, but it affected his memory. When I was a kid, he'd forget to pick me up from friends' houses, or from school when I had to stay late. Once, when I was fourteen, he dropped Coop and I off at Valleyfair to ride the rollercoasters for the day and forgot to come back for us. Eddy finally showed up at ten-thirty that night, and boy was she pissed.

He missed birthdays, school activities, and sometimes entire days at a time. He was always very apologetic, and each time he promised to never let it happen again. And it didn't, until the next time, and the time after that.

After his Navy stint, Dad worked on the Mississippi as an able-bodied seaman, a deckhand on various towboats. That was until his leg got so bad that he had trouble navigating the decks. Then he worked on loading and unloading barges at numerous shipping terminals up and down the Twin Cities corridor.

When he finally quit all together, he bought the Leprechaun, a run-down bar in Northeast Minneapolis. He was in devil's heaven, his beloved booze surrounding him all day, every day.

My dad worked hard to turn a profit, and he really tried to curb his alcohol consumption … until That Night—as I'd come to think of the horrific evening that ended mom's and Eddy's sons' lives and nearly did me in. I still find it hard to look at the jagged scar that starts near my navel and ends just above my right hip bone. If Eddy hadn't literally held me together as we waited for help, three people would have died that night. Eddy had been my lifesaver in so many ways.

Dad struggled mightily for a long time after that, juggling single-handedly raising an in turns rambunctious then withdrawn then out-of-control kid while running the Leprechaun. He turned to Eddy, my mother's closest friend, for help with me and then focused his attention on the bar and the emotional relief he found in Stoli, Jack Daniels, and Brennan's Irish.

Dad and I have a love/hate relationship. I love him, and he loves me. I hate what alcohol does to him, and he hates the fact that I'm an unrepentant lesbian. We try not to talk about either of those issues; when we do, one of us usually storms off in a week-long huff.

This was one visit where my problems had nothing to do with either touchy topic, and I knew he'd jump at the chance to talk about his days on the water.

Coop and I lowered Dawg to the garage floor near midnight, and we all piled into the pickup once again, Dawg tucked between us.

I pulled up to the curb half a block from the bar and cracked a window for Dawg, who, after a halfhearted whine of protest at being left behind, flopped across the bench seat. We strolled to the front door of the Lep and stepped back into another era.

My father decorated the walls of his bar with items he'd collected from a lifetime on the water, including old buoys, cracked oars, and faded pictures going all the way back to his own father's logging days. Dark, exposed beams ran the length of the low ceiling, and a hand-carved wooden bar stood along one side. Lights mounted at intervals on the walls gave the interior a comfortable but not quite cozy feel. Tables were scattered throughout, and three booths at the rear were empty. Cigarette smoke and beer had long ago mixed together to form the familiar aroma bars achieve after years of use and abuse. For the most part, the clientele were blue collar, hard-drinking, hard-working, honest men and women.

I'd spent many hours here as a kid and tended bar as an adult, and I was well-known to most of the regulars. As soon the door shut behind us, one of the men at the bar, a Paul Bunyan with a beard gone wild yelled, "If it ain't Little O'Hanlon!" He hiked himself off his stool, and squashed me in a bear hug. "How ya doin'?" He ruffled my hair, and in a blink I was twelve again.

"Fred," I gasped as I pounded him on the back both in greeting and in an attempt to make him put me down. "I'm good. How's Viva?" His wife was recently diagnosed with breast cancer.

I was deposited on my feet. He said, "Mama's holding her own. The chemo's done and now the docs are doing radiation. They say things are looking pretty good. She's a little lopsided, but she's alive. That's all that matters to me."

"You tell her to hang in there. Dad here?"

Another swat of his big paw slammed my shoulder like a sledgehammer. "He's in back, I think."

I excused myself and dragged Coop along the length of the bar, past four other customers I didn't recognize. Johnny, the bartender, was caught up in conversation with two patrons. I led Coop through a swinging door at the end of the bar that opened into a bright kitchen. Seeing no one, I went to another door that led into the main liquor storeroom. A set of narrow, steep stairs descended into a cellar used to store wine and excess booze. I hollered down the stairs, "Dad!"

My father's voice echoed. "Shay? Be up in a minute, honey." In less than that, he limped up the worn wooden steps with a case of alcohol on his shoulder. At sixty-five, my father was still a handsome man, and again I wondered why he hadn't remarried after my mother's death. But deep down I knew his love for her and his pain over her death held him at arm's length from any woman who entertained thoughts of ending his bachelorhood.

With a heave my dad swung the case of bottles off his shoulder onto a stainless-steel counter. He hugged me, dwarfing me with his burly body and squeezing me with arms that were still rock-hard. He pulled back and stared at me with wide-set green eyes, mirrors of my own. "What are you doing here at this time of night?"

Before I had a chance to answer, Dad released me and caught a glimpse of Coop standing in the doorway behind me. "Nick Cooper, long time no see. You still a vegetable muncher?"

Coop laughed. He'd always gotten along with my dad, especially in the smoking department. That was his saving grace, because my father usually didn't have time for what he termed pansy-assed vegetarians, who, in his book, were barely a step above flaming fags, as he liked to call all homosexuals, occasionally including his own daughter.

"Yeah," Coop said, and gave my father his lopsided grin.

My father's thick, red-fading-to-white hair was freshly shorn, and I was happy to see he was taking care of himself. "What brings you to my neck of the woods?"

"We were wondering if we could hit you up with some questions about shipping on the Mississippi."

Hoisting the box of booze back to his shoulder, he said, "Sure. Give me a minute to put this away, and I'll meet you in a booth in back."

Coop and I settled ourselves in one of the empty booths. Coop lit a cigarette and inhaled deeply. A state-wide smoking ban had gone into effect, but my father couldn't be bothered with something as trivial as forcing his patrons to smoke outside. I was waiting for the cops to slap a fine on him, and then I'd sit back and watch the fireworks from a safe distance. The old man was hard-headed as hell. Some claimed his kid was the same way, but I was too stubborn to agree.

The low tones of an old sixties classic trickled through the speakers dangling from the ceiling and mixed with the quiet drone of conversation.

Dad spoke with Johnny for a minute, and then my father proceeded to restock the storage area under the bar. Johnny mixed up a Fuzzy Navel I knew was meant for me and popped the top off a Bud earmarked for Coop.

He meandered to the booth with drinks in hand. "Where you been lately, Little O?" Johnny always made me smile. He'd started working for my father before he'd been legal to drink and kept the job as he made his way through college. I told him, "Been busy, you know how people want their caffeine fix. How's school?"

His brown eyes gleamed at me. "Same old, ya know? Another year and a half."

I nodded. Johnny was a hard worker and more dependable than most. My dad appeared and slid into the seat beside me with a tumbler of clear liquid I knew was vodka, his late-night drink of choice.

Johnny wandered back to his realm behind the bar. My father lit an unfiltered Camel and exhaled a blue-tinged cloud of smoke. "What do you want to know about the river?"

I cleared my throat, and the end of Coop's cigarette glowed bright as he took another deep hit. Some help he was. I said, "We're trying to track down a shipment that's supposed to be going out tomorrow night. We're hoping you'd have some insight as to which company would most likely store the goods we're looking for."

My father's bushy eyebrows met in a confused frown as the Camel came to his lips again. He rubbed his other hand on top of his bristly head, and I could hear the faint brush of hair against the palm of his hand. "What kind of stuff's headed down the river? That'd be the logical place to start."

"Nuts," I told him. "Almonds." I sipped at my drink. It was strong, and it was good.

"What are nuts doing around here? That's usually a coastal thing. West Coast, I think."

"We're not quite sure," Coop said in a cloud of smoke. Ugh, I was stuck in a pollution sandwich. "We think we have it narrowed down to Ribau Containers, Packer Industries, and the Grizzly Terminal & Dock. At least those are the shipping terminals we could find on the Web that deal with dry goods."

My dad nodded. "Nice job. Ribau? Probably not. They mostly specialize in grains." He flicked cigarette ash in the ashtray, picked up the tumbler, and took a swallow. "Packer won't handle food anymore, only dry stuff like rocks and sand. That leaves Grizzly. They've always been a bit shady, and I'm guessing these nuts of yours aren't exactly a regular shipment, so to speak. Nuts." He shook his head. "What's your interest in this?"

Coop and I shot a look at each other. If my father knew what had happened to Eddy, he'd go ballistic. I never knew if it was honest emotion or macho posturing, but if anyone hurt someone close to my dad, he stormed off to confront the source, and sometimes it ended up uglier than it had started. Now that I thought about that, it sounded kind of familiar.

Making things up on the fly was becoming my strong suit. "Coop thinks one of his friends is involved with this nut shipment.

The guy disappeared two days ago and no one's seen him. We're trying to retrace his steps—before the nuts ship. He told Coop he thought the nuts are being trucked here and then sent off down the Mississippi for resale somewhere else on the black market."

"Isn't that a police issue?" my dad asked, stubbing out his smoke.

Tilting an almost empty bottle at my father, Coop said, "Yeah, but my friend ran into some trouble through the Green Beans. He's on probation. If he's not mixed up in this, and he's on a long bender somewhere, great, his probation officer doesn't need to know about it. If he's really in trouble, well, I doubt that would go over very well with his PO either. The thing is, he's really a great guy, big heart, but he's fallen into some really rough times lately."

Nice job, Mr. Cooper. My dad could certainly relate to self-inflicted bad luck.

"Do you know anyone who works for Grizzly anymore?" I asked and held my breath.

The near-empty glass of Stoli rolled slowly back and forth between my father's palms as he thought about it. "George Unger. He's in charge of keeping the books now that he's off the water. I'm sure he'd be able to look up outgoing shipments."

"Do you think he'd talk to us? Tonight?" I said.

"Tonight?" My father frowned. "It's almost twelve-thirty."

Coop said, "Yeah. The sooner we can figure this out for my friend, the better."

I prayed my father would acquiesce. He stroked his chin, fingertips scraping salt-and-pepper whiskers. "He does owe me from last night's poker fiasco. Bastard screwed me out of a hundred bucks. It'd serve him right to roust him away from his online poker game. Hell, he's a night owl." He stared first at me, and then at Coop. "You sure you can't wait till morning?"

I said the one thing guaranteed to remove any resistance from my father. "Please, Pops?"

Hi eyes narrowed on me. "Christ. Pull that 'Pop' stuff on me and you know I can't say no. I suppose I can call the marker in."

———

The starlit darkness of the night pressed in against the windows of the pickup as we waited in the parking lot of Grizzly Terminal & Dock Company. Out of our sight, the Mississippi silently flowed behind a sprawling, half-moon shaped, corrugated-metal Quonset hut. It reminded me of a gigantic, old-fashioned aircraft hangar. Almost as long as a city block, the building had two big rolling doors that faced us with another door on the far left. We couldn't see the side of the building that faced the water, but I imagined there'd be docks and more big doors, and various pieces of equipment that would be used for loading heavy objects.

My father had gotten a hold of George Unger and successfully conned him into meeting us at the terminal on the southwest edge of the Twin Cities metro area. I had seen George a few times at the Leprechaun when he was playing poker in the back with my father and the other river rats, but that had been years ago, when I was a kid. I vaguely remembered him as a boisterous, friendly man, his face carved with lines from the sun and wind.

He'd instructed my dad to tell us to wait for him in the parking lot, and he'd be on his way after he was finished playing what Dad called another losing hand of five-card stud. George wasn't known for his luck at much of anything.

The engine ticked as it cooled. Dawg was sandwiched happily between me and Coop, his tummy full of two gas station sausage and pepperoni pizza slices. I absently stroked his floppy ear, and he heaved great sighs every couple of minutes. I was sitting next to a stolen dog and a law-dodger, waiting to talk to the numbers man of a shipping outfit that was known more for what it shouldn't involve itself in than for what it had. The worst part was the knowledge that the seconds continued their relentless countdown for Eddy's health and well-being. I hoped, in less than twelve hours, this entire ordeal would be a nightmare ripe for forgetting.

"I need a smoke," Coop said.

"Outside. You just sucked up at the bar. You have issues, dude."

Coop flashed his teeth at me and then groaned as headlights shone in the rear-view mirror. "So much for that idea," he grumbled.

The headlights swept the gravel parking lot as a big, early-nineties Caddy swung around and parked next to us. The lights went out, and we all scrambled from our respective vehicles, except for one suddenly unhappy canine who was getting tired of being left behind.

George looked as I remembered him, with a few years added to a muscular body that was starting to soften around the edges. A comb-over that had seen better days sparsely covered the bald spot on top of his head.

"Little O, been a long time since I laid eyes on you," George said. "You look good, from what I can see in the dark."

"Thanks for coming this late, and on such short notice, George," I said. "This is my friend Nick Cooper."

The two men shook hands, and George led us toward the front door. Over his shoulder he said, "I was up anyway. And make sure you keep this under your hat. My boss wouldn't be too happy to hear I was opening up in the middle of the night to pay back a gambling debt. On top of it, there's been some battles between the terminals around here with one trying to outbid another for shipping jobs, and it's gotten a might dirty." What he left unsaid was that Grizzly was probably the dirty-deal maker.

George unlocked the door and flipped a light switch, illuminating a lobby that had seen better days. Three chairs sported torn brown Naugahyde, and the tan linoleum on the floor was dark with ground-in dirt. The air smelled of diesel, grease, stale cigarette smoke, and something unpleasant that I couldn't quite put my finger on. We followed George down a narrow hall into a postage-stamp-sized office.

The only chair in the room was behind a desk that overflowed with accounting books and various invoices. A bookshelf across from the desk was so loaded with ledgers and three-ring binders that the shelves were permanently bowed.

George settled himself in the chair and we explained what we were hunting for, along with the story of our hard-luck friend. He plucked an olive colored register from beneath a stack of papers, tugged a pair of reading glasses from a shirt pocket, and perched them on his nose. It always amazed me how unorganized people had a way of knowing exactly where things are in their piles of chaos.

"One day I'll get me a secretary," George muttered as he flipped to the page he wanted. He ran a thick finger down hastily scrawled entries, mumbling to himself. "Ah. Here's a load of perishables that came in yesterday. Almonds," he read.

Be still my beating heart.

"Who's shipping them?" Coop asked.

"Says here Riley Derby Inc. out of Brooklyn Park." George squinted up over his glasses at us. "Is that what you want to know?"

"Yeah." I said, nodding, as I tried to repress an ecstatic shout. After all the crap we'd been through, we actually managed to hit some real pay dirt. "When are they supposed to ship?"

George peered through his lenses at the page. "Saturday—tomorrow, or actually I guess that would be today." He paused to frown down at what was most likely a fake Rolex strapped to his wrist. A real one would have been fenced long ago to support his poker-playing lifestyle. "At 8:45 pm."

Yes! That was it. The nuts were within our grasp.

Coop said, excitement evident in his voice, "Where exactly are they stored?"

This time George studied us over his wire rims with a distinct frown creasing his forehead. "Why would you want to know that?"

Coop's mouth snapped shut. It was apparent we'd squeezed as much as we were going to get out of the good Mr. Unger, and if we pushed for any more, he was going to start demanding more answers than we were prepared to give.

I said, "Nevermind Coop. He's got a curiosity streak a mile long. We appreciate the information you've given us."

George slid the glasses off his face and returned them to his pocket. "You tell old Pete the debt's been paid, and I'll see him next Tuesday night."

"I will certainly do that," I said as we followed George out to the lobby and into the dark parking lot. He dug a ring of car keys from his jacket and fished around the pocket again, withdrawing another, smaller set that he used to lock the door.

"Thanks again for coming out here tonight," I said as the gravel covering the parking lot crunched beneath our shoes. "I know it's late." I stepped over one of many ruts in the ground, and my foot caught the edge and came down sideways. I stumbled into George.

"Easy there, Little O!" He quickly reached out to help me right myself as Coop grabbed for my other arm. "This damn lot is a mud puddle when it rains and then it dries uneven, and the company's too cheap to have it graded. One day someone's going to kill themselves and there ain't going to be no more Grizzly, mark my words."

"Thanks for everything, George," I said as I limped to the pickup.

"Next time make it a little earlier, will ya? I have a game to be at. See ya." George called as he crawled into his car and started it. With a wave he wheeled out of the lot.

Dawg's face was pressed against the driver's side window, his wet nose leaving streaks on the glass. His whole body wiggled with excitement as the door opened. Coop pulled the seatbelt across his chest and buckled it as I attempted to do the same, trying to nudge giant dog paws out of the way.

"What now?" he asked.

I grinned at him. "You'll see." I pulled out of the parking lot and watched the taillights of George's car fade in the distance. About two hundred yards down the road, I pulled into an abandoned gas station. I circled the weed-covered building, came to a stop, and flipped the lights off.

"What are you doing?" Coop asked as he strained to see over Dawg, who had decided to perch on his lap and was beginning to pant.

"We're going to make sure the coast is clear, and then we're going back and finding those nuts."

"Come on, the place is locked up tight as a drum."

"Have lock, find key." I held up the key ring George had used to lock the door.

"Where did you—oh. You're bad."

"Hand in, hand out. You know, I never realized it was so easy to pickpocket someone. Maybe we can take that vocation up if this falls through and we have to flee to Mexico."

"What if he comes back?"

"That's why we're waiting. I figure if he doesn't show up within an hour, we're safe to go."

For the next forty-five minutes, we alternated walking Dawg up and down a dense row of trees between the gas station and Grizzly. Between hikes, Coop stood outside the truck and smoked, and I impatiently drummed my fingertips on the steering wheel. I snuck a peek at my watch. 2:33 am. Exhaustion and adrenaline clashed inside my body. If this was what it was like to be James Bond, I wasn't sure I wanted any part of it.

"Okay," I called out the open window. "Let's go see what we can find."

Coop stubbed out his cigarette and herded Dawg into the cab. Once everyone was settled, I cranked the engine and zipped back into the Grizzly lot. I parked in a spot close to some trees and mostly out of sight of the road. We cracked the windows for Dawg, who hung his head as we piled out. Coop gave the mutt a reassuring pat before he closed his door.

We made a beeline for the front door, every step sounding like an explosion in the still night. Wispy clouds partially obscured the moon, making the long building appear even darker and more sinister than before.

I fumbled with the keys while Coop kept watch, and as my patience faded, the correct one slid smoothly into the lock. We slipped inside. Coop closed and locked the door behind us.

I flicked on my flashlight and we headed down the hall, past George's cubbyhole and a couple of other offices. The last door at the end of the hall was closed. As Coop twisted the knob, I said a silent prayer, which someone must have heard, because the door swung open. The beam of my flashlight was dim against the pressing darkness of the surrounding space. *Groundhog Day*, take three.

I swung the light around. It reflected off a number of cargo containers, the kind that can be loaded onto the trailer of a semi or onto railroad cars. They were stacked one atop another in a rusty rainbow of yellows, reds, blues, blacks, and silvers.

Coop stepped through the door and played his own flashlight over the metal crates. "No names on these things, just numbers." He indicated a series of digits painted in white on the side of the container. "There's three, six, nine containers here ... let's see how far down they go."

I followed Coop over to the wall, where a narrow aisle ran between the stacked containers and the corrugated metal siding of the building. We both shone our flashlights down the aisle, and the beams of light were swallowed up by the darkness long before they reached the other end.

I walked past the first mountain of containers. I trudged on for the first three rows, and had a rapidly sinking feeling in my gut. Coop said, "There's got to be a hundred of these things in here. How the hell are we going to figure out which one the nuts are in?"

A ball of desperation clogged my throat, and I swallowed hard. "Maybe the numbers on the containers are linked to that log George had."

Coop grimaced. "That's a lot of numbers."

"You have a better idea?"

"No."

We retreated to George's office. He'd left the shipping log he'd used on the top of the mess on his desk. Coop sat down, and I hovered over his shoulder as he opened the big book and flipped to the last of the entries. The final page showed five different shipments, and they all appeared to be outgoing. Coop's finger ran down to the Riley Derby entry.

"I think it's the right one. Product to be shipped is almonds from California." Coop's finger slid along the page. "They're being transferred in Louisiana to an unnamed shipper. There's letters and numbers after the date. AFIF4101376. Maybe that's the container number."

We jotted the number down, me on my hand and Coop on a Post-It. In my mind, Eddy's voice haunted me yet again, chastising me for writing on my skin, and I shivered. She was forever trying to break me of the habit, and the memory choked me up. I shook off the fear and emotion, turning my attention to our next move.

"Okay, here's what we're going to do," Coop said. He somehow gained strength from each quandary we'd gotten ourselves in and out of during this never-ending night. "We'll each walk alternating rows. If we don't find it the first time, we'll do it again." He stared at me, a fierce gleam in his eyes, the kind of gleam he had when he talked about the latest adventure the Green Beans had embarked on. "Shay, we are going to succeed."

"I know." My voice was much more sure than my heart.

We tramped back out to the cavernous room. Coop took the first row of containers. I took the next. For the next ten minutes, we weaved in a complex dance around each other, flashlight beams bouncing wildly off metal and the rounded interior of the building.

A knot was growing in my stomach, bigger with every non-match my flashlight uncovered. I lost track of how many containers I checked. I plodded past the row Coop was scrutinizing. We were almost to the end of the building. Choking back a frustrated growl, I turned the corner to survey the next stack of rusted metal boxes. When I reached the last set of containers, the space opened into an area the size of a basketball court.

Three semis were lined up, two weighed down with containers, and one empty truck. I shone my light on the first container and stifled an oath when the number didn't match. I sighed and walked to the second truck. About three feet separated the vehicles, making it difficult to see the numbers high above my head, and I had to lean backward to make them out. AFIF4101376. It was a match.

"Coop!" I yelled, frustration forgotten. "Coop, I found it!"

THIRTEEN

Coop came at a run, the beam from his flashlight swinging wildly. He skidded to a stop beside me. "It's on the truck?"

"Yeah!"

Coop's light caught the now familiar numbers painted on the container. "Sweet," he said, excitement bubbling from him like a volcano preparing to blow. "Now what?"

"We take the truck."

"Yeah, right." When I didn't say anything he looked at me. His eyebrows popped up. "Whoa. Wait a minute. I was thinking more along the lines of calling the Bumbling Brothers right now, not embarking on grand theft auto." He eyed the big tractor-trailer. "I mean, grand theft semi."

"We can't do the deal from here, Coop. Dock workers start their days early, like six in the morning early. It's already—" I lit up my watch. "It's 3:14 am. As in Saturday morning. If we don't do something now, the nuts will be floating down the Mississippi, and Eddy will be sunfish niblets."

Coop didn't respond. He closed his eyes and sighed.

"Can you drive this thing?" I asked.

Without opening his eyes, Coop said, "Yeah. I can probably figure it out." He scrambled up and into the cab to check for keys while I headed for a three-by-three foot electrical panel on the wall. We had to get the huge door open so Coop could rumble out with the about-to-be-three-times-stolen cargo.

As I scanned the switches, Coop hollered, "Shay! Keys are here. Where are we going with this monster?"

I rubbed my temples at the ache behind my eyes. "God," I muttered, my mind galloping in circles. "Uh, let's head for the cabin."

"Roger," Coop said. "I'll fire this thing up, and once we're running, you open the door."

"You drive straight out of here and keep on going. You remember where the cabin is, right?"

"Yeah. Can't forget one of the worst hangovers in my life, not to mention that near-drowning."

A little giddy over our sudden progress, I bantered back. "That was your own fault. I told you to stay off the water when you're thirty-three sheets to the wind and it's pitch black out. Start the rig already."

After a long moment of silence, the big vehicle rumbled to life. Coop let it idle for a minute and then gave me the high sign to open the door. I pushed the button, and prayed.

The garage door rumbled up, inch by agonizing inch, coming to a shuddering halt to reveal the opening leading into the cool night. The racket from the door's motor faded, taken over by the low roar of the semi's engine.

Coop eased the monster into the parking lot. He hadn't turned the lights on, and the truck was outlined in black and silver shadow. I ran out, hopped onto the driver's side running board, and stuck my head into the open window.

"You head straight up to the cabin. Don't stop for anything, and for Pete's sake, don't speed."

"I never speed. That's you, honey."

"Be careful. I'm going to close up and head out after you. I shouldn't be more than a few minutes behind."

"Have you got your cell phone?"

I felt for it in my pocket and nodded.

"Call me when you're on the road." Coop reached out and ruffled my hair.

I hopped off the cab, and Coop rolled up the slight incline to the road, paused, and slowly pulled out. The headlights popped on as the truck passed the stand of trees between Grizzly and the abandoned gas station. I watched until the vehicle disappeared out of sight.

My heart was pounding, half in excitement and half in terror of discovery. I couldn't believe we'd pulled it off. We had the nuts, and now all we needed to do was keep them hidden until the meeting with Vincent and Pudge, and then Eddy would be back with us, safe and sound.

I shut the garage door and backtracked, carefully locking up after myself. I left the keys in a mailbox mounted to the building beside the door. Poor George. He'd feel better if he knew he was saving a life.

The oppressive darkness settled around me as I trekked across the lot to my pickup. Even the birds and squirrels must have fallen asleep—no rustling night sounds came from the trees next to the truck. Dawg grinned at me as I got in and gave my cheek a slurp. I scratched the side of his furry face and told him, "It's you and me for a while, pal."

I pulled out of the lot and onto the road, turning on the radio for background distraction. I caught the last bit of Sammy Hagar's distinctive voice as he belted out the final lines of "I Can't Drive 55." I headed north, one hand on the wheel, and the other draped across Dawg's chest as he lay stretched across the seat with his head in my lap.

———

The miles disappeared under my humming wheels as Dawg snoozed and I tried hard not to. I called Coop, and he'd seen two police cars lying in wait on exit ramps, watching for speeders and drunks.

At this late—or was it early?—hour, traffic was light. As I wound my way through the heart of Minneapolis, I was careful to mind my driving manners. The cops were itching for something to do, and I didn't want to provide the something they were doing.

I cleared the city and was soon cruising north on 35W, tapping my fingers against the steering wheel in time to a Nickelback song. I'd felt wide awake when we'd left Grizzly, but as we made it safely through the city, exhaustion tugged at every muscle in my body. My eyelids felt like they weighed ten pounds apiece, and I struggled to keep them open. I resorted to vigorous head shaking, which helped a little, but did nothing to alleviate my headache.

Dawg grunted softly in the grip of some dream, and I rounded the big curve that merged 35W and 35E a few miles south of Forest Lake. Few cars were on the road this far north, and as I came out of the curve, my eyelids inadvertently slid shut again. The wheels hit the warning grooves in the shoulder, sending a loud, thrumming jolt of adrenaline through me, and scaring the bejesus out of Dawg. I swerved in automatic reaction, nearly hitting a car that was passing me on the left. The car stepped on it and squirted past us like a greased piglet.

"Holy shit," I mumbled under my breath and realigned the pickup on the road. Just another thirty minutes and I could collapse for a few hours. I needed to keep it together a little bit longer. Dawg sat stiffly with his front legs splayed wide on the seat. He stared warily at me, his eyes shiny, and one of his eyebrows appeared higher than the other, as if he were questioning my driving abilities. "Gimme a break," I told him. "You try driving a straight line after going through all this crap." He just blinked.

A couple more miles skimmed past. Both sides of the road were now aglow with billboards. As we approached the Forest Lake exit, the Famous Dave's sign shone neon red, and car dealerships lit the night sky. One of the automotive dealers had a gigantic scrolling sign that made me feel like I was in Las Vegas every time I passed it.

A few hundred feet past the exit we plunged back into darkness as street lamps thinned out. I yawned and noticed the flickering of the car lot sign still reflecting red and blue in the cab of the pickup. Odd ... I could still see the strobing lights. I checked the rear-view mirror. My stomach fell to the soles of my feet when I realized that the flashing wasn't coming from one of the signs, but from a police car riding my bumper.

My legs went weak. I had to make a concerted effort to ease onto the brake pedal instead of jamming down on it. Dawg's head whipped toward me when my foot first touched the brake, and he gave me a questioning woof.

"Easy, boy," I muttered, putting a hand on his neck. Here we go, I thought, about to lie to the cops. Again. My track record for honesty in the last twenty-four hours was at an all-time low.

I stopped on the shoulder of the freeway, shifted into park, and groped for the button to roll the window down. The cruiser's bright spotlight reflected off the truck's mirror, effectively blinding me. The seconds stretched painfully as I waited for the police officer to approach my open window. Under my hand Dawg's body started to quiver as he sensed my agitation. The last thing I needed was for him to decide to assert his male dominance and go after the cop. I gripped his collar tight in my fist, the tell-tale tag emblazoned with Buzz's name jingling softly. Thoughts zipped crazily around my head. Did they know about the break-in at the Lazar warehouse? Had they found Luther's body? Had we left some clue as to our identities and they were going to arrest me for murder? Maybe Buzz reported our trespassing on his property and the kidnapping of his dog. Most likely I was about to be arrested for making off with a truckload of stolen nuts.

Just as I was sure I was going to pass out, a flashlight beam shone through the open window into the cab. I attempted to twist around to see the owner of the deep voice that said, "Ma'am, can I see your driver's license and proof of insurance?"

I could barely get turned enough to catch a glimpse of the officer standing behind me as he shone the flashlight directly into my face. He swept it around the interior of the pickup. I blinked against the glare and fumbled in my pocket for the items he requested, which was awkward because I was holding onto Dawg for dear life with my right hand. Dawg bristled but remained still, his ears as far up as they could go. He stared out the window at the cop.

"That's a mighty big dog," the man said as I worked to dig my wallet from my pants.

"Yeah, he is." I managed to wiggle the wallet out of my pocket. I was going to have to let go of that "mighty big dog" to retrieve the identification the officer wanted.

I told Dawg to stay and prayed for the best as I released his collar. With shaking hands I drew out my license and the insurance card.

"Do you know why I pulled you over tonight?"

"Ah—no, sir. Was I speeding?" If only it were that simple. I handed him the items he wanted as white noise roared in my ears.

He was silent a moment as he studied first one piece of identification and then the other, flashlight tucked into one armpit. "No, you weren't speeding. Have you had anything to drink tonight, Ms. O'Hanlon?"

Anything to drink? Oh good god, the man thinks I'm drunk. I struggled to hold back hysterical laughter that threatened to spew forth. At least I wasn't on *America's Most Wanted* yet.

"No, sir, not a drop."

Still studying my identification, he said, "You were swerving all over the road for the last few miles."

"I was? I'm sorry. I guess I'm more tired than I thought."

"Then you won't mind stepping out of the car for a minute, would you?"

Oh Christ. "Yes. I mean no, that's fine. I—"

"Get out of the car."

The officer backed away as I opened the door, keeping tight against the side of my pickup and away from the white line. I climbed out, worried Dawg might try to make a break for it, but he stood on the seat quivering, his eyes tracking my every move.

I followed the cop, who turned out to be a state trooper, to the space between our two vehicles. If a sobriety test was the order of the night, that was great. Then I remembered the cocktail I had at the Leprechaun. But that had been hours ago. It had to have burned out of my system by now. I mentally walloped myself for saying "not a drop."

For the next few minutes, the officer had me watching his finger, walking a line, and balancing on one foot. I was surprised the thumping of my heart didn't knock me off kilter, but somehow I managed to pass all the tests.

"If you'll have a seat in the back, I'll run your license and you can be on your way." The trooper quickly frisked me and deposited me in the back seat of his squad. He settled himself in the front and began to type one-handed on a computer mounted in front of the dash. A digital display in the dashboard read 4:10 am.

The back seat of the cruiser had leg room fit for a midget, and I had to sit sideways. Dim light glowed from the monitor in the front, and the trooper had a reading light attached to it that he held my license under. He slowly entered my information into his computer. I silently chanted come on, come on, come on, as he pecked away at the keyboard, thinking that every minute I was in the officer's presence was another moment he might figure out he had a hot commodity on his hands.

After what felt like hours, he caught my gaze in the rear-view mirror. "You're good to go, Miss O'Hanlon. Next time you're feeling sleepy, do us all a favor and pull over and take a nap."

My ID returned, I was sprung from the back seat. My legs were weak as I crawled into the pickup beside Dawg, and I breathed a thank-you to the heavens and pulled back onto the road. The lights from the squad slowly faded away. What next? I was beginning to think this night would never end.

FOURTEEN

DAWG AND I ARRIVED at the cabin without further interruption. Coop was sound asleep on the couch, his arm over his eyes and one leg resting on the floor, an old blanket half covering him. I gently tucked it up under his chin.

After a quick trip to the facilities for both Dawg and me and some ibuprofen for my head, I crashed on the bed in my room. Dawg nudged his way into the blankets. Then he groaned and heaved himself onto his side, curled one monster front paw against me, and plopped the other across my chest. His big head took up half my pillow, but I was too tired to care.

Sleep slammed into me. I didn't know how long I'd been floating in blissful nothingness when an obnoxious ringing startled me into semi-consciousness. I nearly fell off the bed groping for the source of the sound. Dawg had wiggled even closer to me, and I occupied about a foot of mattress at the edge of the bed.

The objects in the room were no more than dim outlines in the weak light that seeped around the edges of the drawn blinds. Finding the familiar shape of my cell phone, I grabbed it and squinted at the front readout. It was a number I didn't recognize.

I flipped the phone open as Coop popped into the doorway, sleepy and panicked at the same time.

"Hello?" My voice was husky from sleep, or lack thereof.

"Is this Shag O'Hanlon?" A woman's cultured voice sounded vaguely familiar, but I couldn't place it through the sleep-fog in my brain.

"Shay, yes."

"You have something of ours. Actually two somethings. We want them back, you lying little Minnesota Storage Facility Inspector's Office bitch." The voice faded from cultured to gritty in a breath. Rita Lazar.

"Ah," I choked out.

Ignoring my gurgle, Rita continued, "I don't know what the hell you're up to, but we want that truck you heisted last night, and Buzz wants that ugly dog of his back, too. Don't ask me why. It's a disgusting, slobbering thing."

"Ah," I tried again. "But—"

"There's no buts here, you conniving thief. We get what we want, and we'll give you this in return." A moment of silence was broken by scuffing sounds in the background. A distant voice said something in a very unfriendly tone, and then, "Shay O'Hanlon? Shay O'Hanlon, Ms. Rita's fallen off her rocker. Help me, Shay O—" The voice was abruptly cut off and Rita came back on the line.

"Yes, Shay O'Hanlon," she mimicked. "You have to help widdle Rocky."

161

Any remaining vestiges of sleepiness vanished the moment I heard Rocky's voice, and fury instantly replaced confusion. My body began to vibrate with anger. "Don't you—don't you dare hurt him, Rita," I shouted into the receiver. "He's done nothing to you."

No way could there be two kidnappings in my mundane life. It wasn't possible. Then Rita cackled in my ear, assuring me I wasn't in the grip of some incomprehensible dream. She sounded more convincing than the Wicked Witch of the West ever did.

"The nuts—" she began but was interrupted by someone, probably Buzz. Then she continued with an exasperated breath, "and that disgusting dog will buy freedom for our dear friend Rocky." Her voice dripped with sarcasm. "You have the nuts and the dog at the Grizzly terminal at—" she was again interrupted by Buzz. "Four this afternoon. Not a moment later. Got that?" Without waiting for a reply, she hung up on me. I sat a full minute staring disbelievingly at the phone in my hand, and then slowly flipped it shut.

"Now what?" Coop asked.

Still staring at the phone, wondering how things could have gone from dire to insane, I murmured, "I can't believe it. Rita and Buzz snatched Rocky and they'll trade him for the truck and Dawg." I blinked slowly. "How on earth did we get involved in not one, but two kidnappings? Oh, excuse me," my voice started to raise, barely held back hysteria about to let loose. "I meant two kidnappings, a dognapping, a stolen truck, and a dead body. Oh, and I got pulled over for drunk driving on the way up here." I shook my head, attempting to pull myself back from the brink. "Makes lying to the cops about *your* whereabouts pretty minor, doesn't it?"

Coop peered at me with a mixture of fear and concern. Even Dawg was awake now, his eyes wide, his forehead wrinkled as if he understood the tension and emotion in the air. He huffed at me, then leaned forward and gently licked my forearm.

"I'm so confused. Are Rita and our mobsters in cahoots? Oh lord," I flopped back onto the pillow.

"Who the hell knows. Doesn't seem like it, but I suppose they could be."

The display on my cell read 7:10 am. We were supposed to call Vincent at one o'clock for further instructions. Now this. Oh Eddy. I swallowed back a sob that came out like a hiccup.

Coop sighed deeply. "Shay, everything's going to be okay. Let's just think this through. Two sets of crazies want this godforsaken truck with its stupid nuts and we need to figure out a way to make them both happy. And they may or may not be working together."

"If they're not, how did Rita and Buzz figure out what we were up to?" My voice was muffled beneath the hand I'd thrown over my face.

"I suppose they know Rocky hangs with me sometimes, and they got your name from your visit to Rita. They may have asked Kate how to get a hold of you. Or maybe Rocky knew the number." We both cringed, knowing how hard it was for us to pry information out of Rocky. For Buzz and Rita to have gotten anything out of him, they would have had to use some seriously persuasive and probably painful techniques.

"And Buzz and his pal saw you and me at his junkyard," Coop continued.

I moaned, and Dawg whined.

"Come on, be quick and make me some breakfast." Coop ducked out of the way of the pillow I threw at his head and dragged me to my feet.

———

The cabin was a cozy affair with two bedrooms, a rustically decorated living room complete with a fireplace and mantle, and a cheery kitchen painted canary yellow with rust trim. As much as Dad and I loved our bucolic setting, he appreciated his creature comforts. Both bedrooms and the living room had TVs and DVD/VCR combos to help pass cold winter evenings, and the cabin was wired with high-speed Internet, which Dad hated and I loved. I rarely had free time at home, so the setup was a bit of a guilty pleasure for me.

Exposed log beams made up the walls throughout the structure and I ran a hand over the glossy blond wood. As I stood in the doorway between the kitchen and living room, the immediate situation faded as usually repressed memories washed over me in nostalgic monsoon.

The property had been in the family longer than I'd been around, and in my mind's eye, I could still smell the suntan lotion my mother slathered on me before I splashed a hot summer's day away in the lake. I could still feel her soft hands as they slid across my skin, making sure to cover every exposed inch. The memories I had of her and this place were filled with unconditional love. God, I missed her.

The cabin was a refuge. When I was lost, hurting, and lonely, when life's pressures overwhelmed me, this was where I hid until I regained my equilibrium. This was the place where memories of a happier time always swept over me, where I could still feel the pull of my mother. These walls meant safety and love, security and peace. But this time, I realized as I dragged myself out of my reverie, this cabin was an honest-to-goodness escape.

Coop and I quickly scrounged up some breakfast and bounced ideas off of each other as we ate. Neither of us came up with any miraculous solutions. I finished off my bowl of instant oatmeal, the apple and cinnamon flavor stuck in the back of my throat, and crossed the kitchen to the sink. I scooped up the bowl we'd given to Dawg, and it turned out he liked instant oatmeal as much as Subway sandwiches and pizza. I wondered if he'd even entertain the idea of regular dog food after this. He lay quietly in the corner, his lips draped on either side of the paws his head rested on. His shiny eyes continually flicked from Coop to me and back.

Coop grabbed a towel and dried our few dishes. "Shay, it's time to call JT. I know I suggested this before, but this time I really think we should. She did tell you to call her if you were in trouble, and you are—*we* are—in some deep-ass shit." He carefully dried the spoons and tucked them in the silverware drawer. "Long ago this stopped being about me," he added. "I can see that now."

"What if Vincent finds out we went to the cops?" I asked.

"We have to hope he doesn't."

"This sucks."

"I've got it!" A devilish expression appeared on Coop's face. "How about we steal another truck with a rusty container, deliver it to the junkyard, and hope Buzz doesn't open it up before we get out of there with Rocky. Then we go Eddy hunting."

I swallowed a snort. "And where do you propose we find a truck that would fit the bill? Go back to Grizzly and swipe another one? I can see it now. 'Oh, George, we need to borrow another truck for a few hours. We promise we'll give it back.'" I rolled my eyes. "He'd probably have us arrested on sight. My dad's going to kill us when George tells him what we did."

The humorous expression on his face faded. "God, Shay, I hope Eddy's okay."

I nodded somberly. "Me too."

We finished the dishes and returned to the table. Reluctantly, I pulled out JT's card and punched her number into my cell. By the fourth ring, I was almost hopeful she wasn't going to answer. I was about to hang up when I heard a click and then a cold, hard voice uttered, "Bordeaux."

Words caught in my throat, and for a second I couldn't get anything out.

"Hello?"

"JT—it's Shay. Shay O'Hanlon."

The voice warmed instantly. "Shay, it's good to hear from you. You weren't at the Hole this morning."

So she'd stopped by again. I wondered if it was because she was after me, if she was simply in love with Kate's drink-making abilities, or if she was still sniffing around for Coop. Maybe it was all of the above.

I took a deep breath and exhaled fast. "JT, okay, there's something I need to talk to you about." I caught Coop's eyes and he nodded, silently encouraging me. "Is there any way you can meet up with me this morning? It's kind of an emergency."

Stillness reigned on the other end of the line and seconds felt like minutes. Then, "Of course. Where?"

Why did I not think things through beforehand? Where? Here? No. My mind raced. "There's a Denny's right off 35 in North Branch. Can you meet me there in an hour?"

More silence, then JT said, "No problem. I'll be there. Should I come alone?"

"Yeah. Alone would be good."

"I'll be there," JT repeated. Then she quietly asked, "Are you okay?"

The kindness in her voice nearly made me lose what tenuous self-control I still possessed. With effort I swallowed the ball of emotion that blossomed in my throat. "Yeah," I whispered, and hung up before I completely lost it.

———

At a quarter to nine, we made a quick trip to the North Branch post office to mail a copy of Kinky's video that we'd made to the address on JT's business card. We didn't want the bad guys getting away in the—don't even think it, Shay!—event things didn't work out like they were supposed to.

Coop and Dawg waited in an adjacent business' parking lot as I sat in a booth at Denny's. The building was a Fifties-styled diner, complete with sparkly red-vinyl seats, lots of chrome, and a jukebox in the corner. I thanked the waiter when he handed me a Cherry Coke, impatiently thrumming my fingers on the retro tabletop. The aroma of coffee and French toast made my stomach rumble.

Coop and I had decided I'd meet JT alone to drop the bomb on her. Actually, multiple bombs. I had visions that alternated between JT arresting me on the spot and her hightailing it out of the diner without a backward glance.

The door swung open and JT strode inside. She paused long enough to slip the sunglasses from her eyes to their usual spot on top of her head. She squinted, scanning the narrow room. Glossy hair hung in loose waves at her shoulders, unleashed in all its glory from the ponytail in which it was usually bound.

"What's the emergency?" JT asked as she slid into the booth, her dark eyes narrowed on me, her face unreadable. I resisted the urge to squirm. Now or never.

"Okay, here's the—" As I was about to spew the sordid tale, my cell rang. I gave JT an apologetic look and palmed it. A phone number I didn't recognize was displayed on the readout. A sharp moment of wariness poked me in the gut, and I momentarily considered not answering. However, the stakes of the game were way too high not to.

"Excuse me," I said to JT as I slipped from the booth and headed toward the exit, flipping the phone open as I walked. "Hello."

The voice on the other end of the line stopped me in my tracks before I made it out the door, and simultaneously sucked the air right out of my body.

"Girl, where the hell are you? You gotta come and rescue my plump behind!"

"Eddy? Eddy?!" My voice went up a number of octaves as I repeated her name.

"Shay, you listen to me, girl. I'm at the World Market Square in the old Sears building on Lake. Don't know how much time I have before those two nincompoops come poking around, and you need to get me before they do. They gonna be two mad 'nappers when they wake up."

I was having a hard time keeping up. "Eddy! You—"

Eddy cut me off. "Child, you get over here and rescue these old bones. I can't keep hiding out in a bathroom, again. I don't dare go outside. I'll be by the restroom next to a tent where some shyster's telling fortunes. They ought to get Hazel working there. She knows what she's talkin' about. Gotta go." Before I could reply, Eddy was gone.

My mouth hung open for a number of seconds, and the waiter, the cook, and JT all stared at me. I managed a chagrined face for the staff and made a split second decision. In three long strides, I was at the table. Hand in pocket scraping for change, I came up with a five, tossed it on the table and grabbed JT's arm. "Come on," I said. She stared at me as if I'd lost my mind, probably trying to decide if she dared follow this lunatic or not. Then she slid from the booth and nearly fell on her face as I dragged her toward the door. We burst out of the restaurant, cut through parked cars and across a grassy median that separated parking lots. JT didn't say a word as I pulled her across the asphalt toward my pickup.

Coop saw us coming fast, and he opened the door and stepped out of the truck. As we bore down on him I yelled, "Make room for JT. Crawl in back." The Dakota had an extended cab, with a miniscule bench seat in the rear. If a body could fold up like an accordion, as Coop's could, it worked. He opened his mouth to speak, but the expression on my face shut him up. He scrambled into the tiny space, coaxing a now panting Dawg in next to him.

JT watched Coop and Dawg's quick version of musical chairs and, to her credit, did not decide we were crazy enough to arrest or scary enough to bail on.

"Get in," I barked at her. I crawled inside and slammed the door. She hesitated, obviously processing another internal debate. Decision made, she walked around the front of the truck and climbed in. I yanked at my seatbelt and cranked the ignition.

Tires squealing, we peeled out of the lot and followed a secondary road to the entrance of the freeway. In moments, we were flying along the interstate at eighty miles an hour.

Dawg sniffed JT with his lip-stuck-on-tooth thing going on again. "Do you want to tell me what the hell this is all about?" she asked.

I took a gulp of air, blew it out through pursed lips, and hazarded a peep at her. Most of her was blocked by Dawg as he energetically welcomed her into his new pack. Both of her hands were on either side of Dawg's head, rubbing his jowly cheeks, trying to keep his bouncing tongue from slobbering on her more than he already had. I gently put a hand on the top of his head and pulled him away from JT's face. Coop sat frozen in back, and from the rear-view mirror he shot me a what-do-you-think-you're-doing glare.

"First off, JT, I guess you should say hello to Dawg."

She ducked away from another swipe of Dawg's tongue and peered over his head at me. "Didn't know you had a dog."

"I didn't, ah, until very recently. He's part of this long story we need to tell you. And, behind you is the elusive Nick Cooper. Coop, this is JT."

JT tried to peer over Dawg at Coop and settled on a simple hello.

"I want you to know that I had nothing to do with Kinky's death," Coop told the back of JT's head.

I had to give JT credit for remaining calm. I didn't know how I'd feel if I was dragged along by someone suspicious, stuck riding in a car alongside a giant drooling canine, with a person who was wanted for questioning in a murder case sitting behind me. Instead of pulling her gun on us, she said, "I know."

I wasn't sure if I'd heard her correctly. "You know? What do you know?"

"I know Mr. Cooper didn't kill Stanley Anderson."

"Coop," Coop said.

"But—you kept showing up asking me if I knew where he was." JT met my eyes and held my gaze until I had to look back at the road in front of us.

She quietly said, "I never said he murdered Stanley Anderson. We told you we had some questions to ask him."

I thought back to that first conversation, and what JT claimed was indeed true. They never did accuse Coop of anything.

"Why were you searching so hard for me, then?" Coop asked.

"First, we always question the entire staff when there's a homicide at a workplace, and second, we thought you might have knowingly, or unknowingly, been witness to some of Mr. Anderson's underhanded dealings." JT sighed and ran her fingers through her hair. "We've been investigating the man for the last six months."

"The last six months?" Coop said, surprise evident in his tone.

"Yes."

171

"For what?" I figured maybe it had something to do with selling sleazy amateur porn.

"Various stuff. We're pretty sure he was in cahoots with the Mafia, using Pig's Eye Bingo to launder mob money. And your boss was up to his eyeballs in a few other nefarious deals. He's probably a small fish, but the investigation was progressing nicely until he got himself killed. We retrieved the video from his office, but nothing on it pointed to the killer. Your prints, Coop, were on the murder weapon, but you work at the bingo palace, and that was to be expected. The one very interesting set of prints came back to a known member of the Massioso crime family out of New Jersey."

My fingers tightened on the wheel. "His name wasn't Pudge, was it?"

JT shot me a look. "His name is Theodore Mahoney, but he goes by Pudge. If you want to get really sick, his crime family nickname is Pudge the Package."

"The Package?" I grimaced.

She nodded. "Yup. He's rumored to have some sizeable family jewels."

"Ugh. Stupid question. I did not need to know that."

"Anyway. We've been hunting for him and another member of the crime family named Vincent Ragozzi."

"Oh," I said, amusement slipping away like a phantom as the weight of JT's words sunk in. I caught Coop's gaze through the rear-view mirror. "We were right, Coop. Eddy was kidnapped by the mob after all."

JT stiffened. "Kidnapped? Who's been kidnapped?"

With Coop throwing in his two cents now and then, I filled JT in on the events of the previous day and night. I told her about Eddy's kidnapping, our investigations, Lazar's unfortunate demise, Dawg's decision to follow us, a very abbreviated version of the borrowing of the nuts, and the subsequent abduction of Rocky. There'd be time later for full confessions, as soon as Eddy and Rocky were safe and sound.

JT nodded thoughtfully as she said, "I assume you're coming to the part where you get a phone call and drag me out of Denny's."

"Oh, holy crap! How could I forget? Jesus. That was Eddy. She's okay! We have to get to her before Pudge and Vincent find her."

I merged onto 94 and whizzed around a UPS truck.

"What?" Coop shrieked, leaning as far forward between the seats as he could. "Why didn't you say so?"

"She's at the old Sears building off of Lake. Don't ask me how, but she escaped from Laurel and Hardy and is hiding out by the fortune teller in the World Market Square." I passed a car dawdling along in the right lane and briefly wondered if a cop could ticket someone for speeding when they were a passenger in the car.

"Un-freaking-believable," Coop said.

"She okay?" JT asked.

"I think so. She was her usual feisty self, anyway." It was when Eddy went quiet that you knew you were in deep crap.

"I should call this in—" JT said as she flipped her cell phone open.

A moment of hysteria seized me. "NO!" I interrupted her as panic blossomed like a mushroom cloud. "JT, wait. We don't know—"

173

Coop butted in, surfing my urgency. "Please, JT. Vincent explicitly said they'd kill Eddy if we called the cops. What if they get to her before we do and then the cops show up? Those two are obviously ruthless. Who knows what they'd do."

JT sighed, stared out the window, and slowly snapped her phone shut. Then she said, "I can't believe I'm going along with this. It's so against my better judgment. But if things get even the slightest bit hinky, I'm on the phone before you can say a word."

I was grateful for her understanding, regardless of how tentative that understanding might be. We rode in a heavy silence for a couple of minutes.

Then she said, "So. These nuts you 'borrowed.' Where are they, exactly?"

"At my dad's cabin, safe and sound. Once we retrieve Eddy, we need to run back up and get them. Then it's Rocky's turn for freedom." I alternated between outrage at Rita and Buzz and fear at the thought of what they may have done to Rocky. Innocent Rocky, who wanted nothing more than to feel needed and to eat at Popeye's. JT pulled me back into the moment when she said, "I knew something was up last night when I caught up with you behind the Rabbit Hole."

My face grew hot, and my ears burned.

"I wish you'd have told me what was going on," she said.

Coop leaned between the seats. "We didn't dare. First of all, those yahoos threatened to kill Eddy if we didn't cough up the nuts. Then we figured you were ready to haul me in and throw away the key. Shay was trying to protect both of us."

Ah, my tarnished knight, standing up for me again.

A smile tugged at the corners of JT's mouth. "You do have quite the record, Mr. Greenpeace."

"Yeah, I know. Only for good causes, though."

"We need a plan. Who's got a plan?" I asked.

JT said, "We get Eddy and then deal with Rita and Buzz." She drew out her cell phone and flipped it open. "What are Buzz and Rita's last names?"

Dread and fear thundered back into my consciousness. "You said you weren't going to call this in."

JT's drilled me with hard cop eyes. "I gave you my word. When I say something, I mean it, Shay. I want to run these bozos and see what comes back. So we know what we're getting into, okay? And I need to talk to Tyrell so we can figure out the best way to attack this mess."

"Okay, okay." Consider me spanked.

"She's just worried about Eddy and Rocky," Coop told her.

I gave her the names, and we rode in silence as JT um-hmmed and uh-huhed into her phone. Tyrell's voice rumbled in reply through the cell's earpiece, but I couldn't make out any of his words. She disconnected with a sigh.

"What's he say?" I snuck long peeks at her profile as she stared out the windshield.

"Buzz has a long record that includes assault, petty theft, a grand theft auto charge that was tossed on a technicality, and some other minor stuff. Rita comes back clean."

"Doesn't surprise me," Coop said. "He's a first-class jerk."

"We're all going to meet up with Tyrell at two o'clock and we'll map out a plan of action."

From the back seat, Coop leaned forward again. "I think Buzz's running a chop shop out of that junkyard in Brooklyn Park."

I tuned out Coop and JT as they discussed the finer points of chopping and swapping, my mind focusing on Eddy's rescue. Part of me still felt like we were trapped in some kind of psychotic, never-ending nightmare and any second I'd wake up snug in my bed, safe and sound. Eddy would be downstairs puttering around, and Rocky would be visiting people and hoping to score a meal at Popeye's.

FIFTEEN

NEITHER COOP NOR I had been inside the Sears building since it turned into the World Market Square. JT had, but it was some time ago, and she didn't remember any fortune tellers. We trooped up the cement stairs and slipped inside. A mélange of fragrant odors, both pungent and subtle, wafted through the air, making my mouth water. The place was abuzz with shoppers of various nationalities, surging through narrow aisles lined with tiny store-fronts advertising everything from exotic food to textiles from countries around the world. Many secondary aisles shot off the main ones, creating mini neighborhoods.

"I swear this is a maze from hell," JT said. "You have your cell, Shay? Coop?"

I grabbed my phone and flipped it open. Still had half the battery life left. "Coop's got one, too, why?"

"I think we should split up. We'll cover more ground, and who-ever finds the fortune teller calls the others and we'll meet there."

JT took off in one direction, Coop struck out the opposite way, and I took the middle route, hustling past a pizza joint, a Greek eatery, and Cambodian cuisine in rapid succession. I played the bob and weave game as I made my way along, cursing under my breath at shoppers moving at a snail's pace.

The aisle ahead of me opened into an area the size of a high school gym with a stage situated in the center. Five kids gathered around a piñata suspended from the ceiling, taking turns trying to crack the bright green donkey open. One preteen boy, blindfolded with a multi-colored, striped cloth that flowed gracefully around him, took a mighty whack at the piñata. Laughter floated as the club he wielded sliced through empty air, the piñata swaying safely behind his head. His friends howled and shouted unhelpful directions as he took another ineffective swat.

I hurried past, thinking how ironic it was that people could be having such a good time when so much was at stake. I entered another aisle on the far side of the stage. To my right was an East African stand with hundreds of objects carved in wood so dark it was almost black. To my left incense floated from an Indian boutique. No fortune teller. I was about to head down an adjacent aisle when it occurred to me that we were a bunch of idiots. Why didn't we just ask someone where the fortune teller was?

The next stand had Thai, and my stomach rumbled as I stood impatiently behind a chubby mom rooting around the bottom of her handbag looking for her billfold, a squirming kid on her hip. I was about to grab her purse and find it for her when I felt the vibration of my cell phone.

"Yes," I answered.

"I've got her," Coop said. "Where are you?"

Eureka! "I just passed an African place."

"Go toward the windows along the back side of the building, and make a right down the last aisle. I'll call JT." Coop disconnected, and relief shot through my veins, the rush of it was how I imagined cocaine would feel. The shakes set in. I spotted a row of windows at the far end of the aisle and speed-walked through ambling shoppers. I careened around the corner, and nearly crashed into a shabby red-and-black-velvet tent with tassels hanging at each corner. A rough piece of plywood sporting hand-painted white letters announced:

MS. FORTUNA
FORTUNE TELLER
$25 AND THE FUTURE IS YOURS

Eddy, dressed in a black T-shirt emblazoned with the words "Don't Mess With A Knitter," and blue jeans rolled at the cuffs, stood with Coop and JT outside the entrance of Ms. Fortuna's establishment, along with a woman who couldn't be anyone but Ms. Fortuna. She was dressed in a blood-red robe and her dyed ink-black hair was swathed in a filmy purple and scarlet scarf. Deep-set, dark-shadowed eyes peered out beneath a heavy brow.

I flung my arms around Eddy. A lump the size of a grapefruit lodged in my throat as she squeezed me hard. She whispered, "You get yourself together. I'm fine. But you're kind of smelly." She squeezed me again and then stepped away. "You think a couple rotten bad boys could keep me down? Hell no! Took a frying pan to their thick heads while they were sleeping. They should come to a Knitters' meeting to learn how to tie a proper knot."

I tried to unobtrusively sniff my underarm. Yeah, I needed a shower.

Eddy introduced us to Ms. Fortuna, who said in a gravelly voice, "You kids come back any time and I'll do a reading for you. And you," she squinted one black-rimmed eye at Eddy. "Remember what I said, and stay away from the man with bad breath."

Eddy slapped a hand to her chest. "You got it, sister. Thanks for saving me from the bathroom. I'll call you with the next Mad Knitters meeting date." I guess the shyster was okay after all. They did a complicated handshake, one I couldn't even begin to replicate, and we made tracks. I didn't know what kind of magic Eddy had in that heart of hers, but give her ten minutes and she could create camaraderie with anyone.

I was about to hit Eddy up with questions as we hustled along when Coop said, "I'm going to run ahead and let Dawg out before we take off." He bolted before anyone could say a word.

"He's in the throes of a nic fit," I said. "Have you met JT, Eddy?"

"Coop did the honors," JT said.

Eddy turned and leaned conspiratorially into me. "She's a babe, that one." Oh God. Before I had a chance to come up with a reply, we shifted into single file to pass a large group of people milling around an Indian food stand. From somewhere nearby the sounds of a flute floated over the crowd.

Eddy eyed me once we were past the throng. "What dog?" she asked.

Oh boy. I opened and closed my mouth a couple of times. "Ah, yeah, the dog. We kind of adopted a dog, and his name is Dawg. D-a-w-g."

"Huh. Dumb name. Didn't know you wanted a dog. What's he like, a cute, bitty, fuzzy poodle with one of those adorable balls on his tail?"

"Not exactly." Eddy loved animals, but I wasn't sure how she'd take to a pooch the size of a baby moose.

I was about to try to explain Dawg when JT said, "Hey, I'll catch right up. Got to hit the bathroom. Get out to the truck and lock the doors."

JT veered out of the main aisle, making a beeline for a restroom in the distance. Effectively interrupted, I dropped the Dawg conversation.

"Child, you know where you're goin'? I'm confused as all get out in this place. Although," Eddy stared longingly at a food stand hawking aromatic Mexican tamales as we walked rapidly past, "I wouldn't mind coming back when we're not running from Ding and Ling."

As I took a breath to answer her, she squeaked once and froze. I followed her gaze, and at the far end of the long aisle, maybe two hundred feet away, two men dressed in black suits made their way toward us, threading past milling shoppers. One man was tall with slicked-back dark hair and the other was short and round. They looked like a couple of mobsters. I blinked once, then again. They *were* mobsters.

Eddy grabbed my arm as she began backpedaling. "Come on child—that's—"

Before she could utter another word, the tall man stopped for a moment, and our eyes locked. Vincent. We were too far away to hear him clearly, but the words "—old bat! Get her—!" floated clearly through the air. He started plowing his way down the aisle like an out-of-control locomotive, Pudge hot on his heels, both of them shoving unsuspecting people out of their way. Angry customers scowled as the two men bumbled past.

"Run!" Eddy yelled, her usually gravelly voice high-pitched. We backtracked and rerounded the corner that we'd passed moments ago. I searched for JT, but she was nowhere in sight. Bad timing for a potty break. We were on our own.

———

We threaded our way down the crammed aisle, not quite running but moving as fast as we could. I shot a quick look over my shoulder. Pudge and Vincent hadn't made the corner yet. Frantically we scanned the area for a place to hide. We'd dodged down almost half the long corridor when I heard one of the Mafioso's yelling again, and the voice sounded nearer. Vincent and Pudge rocketed around the corner and were closing the gap, paying no heed to people in their way.

Eddy's hand clenched my arm. Without warning she veered off the main drag into one of the many narrower corridors, nearly giving me whiplash. We scrambled around a hot dog shop on the corner and shot past two more food stands.

The path dead-ended about fifty feet ahead. On our left a textile shop, easily double the size of most of the businesses in the Market, displayed hundreds of colorful fabrics. Across from it stood a fresh fish stand, and a fruit and vegetable mini-mart ended the road.

"This way!" I hauled Eddy through the fish seller's storefront. Fishy stench assailed my nostrils. We screeched to a stop in the center of the tiny store, and I nearly wiped out as one of my shoes hit a patch of wet tile next to a big, round live-fish tank. The tank was waist high, filled with a variety of what appeared to be tiny lobsters. Their mini-pincers waved madly about as they waited to be purchased and probably boiled. Without Eddy's steadying hand I would have run right into the side of the huge container and taken a nose dive in with the smelly crustaceans.

A white, refrigerated display case stocked with assorted fish parts sat beside another coffin-sized, glassed-in tank. More live lobsters, much bigger than those in the pool on the floor, shifted around in slow motion within the glass. The proprietor was no-where to be seen, and we ducked out of sight behind the refriger-ated display.

The rumble of pedestrians and shoppers was muted. The air was overly warm and stagnant. Eddy panted beside me, mumbling under her breath. All I could make out between her gasps were whispered comments: *honky bastards*, *goddamn arthritis*, and *pasty white knee-huggers*, whatever that meant. Behind us a swinging door led into what I suspected was a storage room. On my left a three-foot gap separated the refrigerated display we were hiding behind from the lobster coffin.

My heart thumped hard in my chest. With any luck the bum-bling duo would simply stick their heads in the store, see nothing, and continue on their way.

I strained to listen, my eyes locked on the dirty grout in the gray tile floor. Eddy suddenly poked me hard in the side, and I shifted slightly toward her. As I did, a sturdy pair of what old folks might call sensible shoes filled my vision. Nylon knee-highs that had long ago lost their elasticity bunched around a set of thick ankles. Varicose vein-covered calves disappeared beneath the ragged hem of a faded skirt. As I raised my head, I saw two meaty hands propped on wide hips. A stained, off-white apron protected the woman's outfit. Back in the day, she would have had boobs out to there, but now it was boobs down to there. A dark-blue shirt was buttoned up tight under her chin.

The woman's tired, lined eyes peered down at us with a mixture of anger and curiosity. Narrow granny glasses rested on her forehead instead of on her nose, and she'd tucked a piece of wadded up Kleenex under the bridge of the glasses. She scowled at us and then spoke, her voice emanating from below the thick rubber soles of her shoes. "What you doing down there?"

Before I could utter a word, Eddy gave the woman a huge grin. She was charming even on her knees. "Hi there! Don't mind us, we—ah, see, there's these two very bad—" A loud crash, a splash, and a string of oaths from the front of the store stopped Eddy mid-sentence. The woman's head snapped up, and her scowl deepened.

"You clumsy man! You get out of my crawfish right now or I call police."

A familiar voice sounding slightly tinny and very strained rumbled, "OW! Goddamn—UGH!" It sounded like Pudge picked the wrong pool to plop in. He was about to get one serious ass-whooping. More spluttering and more splashing. Then the clack of hard-soled shoes hitting the tile floor echoed in the store.

I was dying to stick my head around the side of the cooler, but restrained myself. As long as the woman didn't give us away, we had a fighting chance.

"Lady, did you see a little old black lady and a taller white girl come by here?" Pudge asked, then mumbled, "Goddamn lobsters. I freaking hate lobster." Unbelievably, Pudge and I had something in common. A soggy slapping sound was followed by a crunch as something hit the floor. "Oh—Christ, that's disgusting. You seen them or not?"

Eddy and I waited for the woman's response. Her face had turned impassive. "Not lobsters. Crawfish, stupid fat man. You owe ten dollars."

"Jesus, what the hell, lady?"

I wondered where Vincent was, wondered if Pudge was distracting the woman so Vincent could get a gander behind the display cases.

The woman raised her arm and pointed over the top of the refrigerated case. "My crawfish. You throw on floor. You break, you buy."

We stared up at the woman.

"I'm not paying you a damn dime." Pudge's voice cracked with anger, or maybe frustration. "It was your fucking wet floor—"

"Ten dollars," she interrupted, her voice rising.

I couldn't help but try to peek around the edge of the case. Pudge stood next to the tank, his head, right shoulder, and right arm were soaked, dripping water on the floor. A nasty lump with a ragged, raw cut adorned one side of his face. Two crawfish lay belly up on the tile by his feet. A third one dangled from the sleeve of his jacket.

Before anyone could say another word, Vincent burst into the store and stopped short when he caught sight of Pudge and his new friends. "What the hell happened to you?"

Pudge's head whipped from Granny Glasses to Vincent and back. I struggled to remain silent. Eddy scooched around behind me, elbowing me in the side, wanting to get an angle on the action. I tried to wave her away, afraid she'd lean out too far.

Water continued to dribble in an ever-growing puddle around Pudge. "I was checking in here when I slipped on some goddamn water and fell into that fucking tank." His face turned redder as each word popped from his mouth. He shook his fist at Granny. "I coulda drowned. I should sue your sorry—"

"Ten dollars." The woman's face remained impassive as she interrupted him again.

With a grimace of disgust, Vincent grabbed Pudge by the dry arm and yanked him toward the exit. "For Christ's sake, come on. We gotta find those two." His voice faded as they made a left out the door and headed down the corridor, leaving a trail of water in their wake. After a couple of seconds, the crawfish that clung tenaciously to Pudge came flying into the shop, bounced off the glass display case, and hit the floor with a juicy splat.

Granny silently watched as Eddy and I rose and dusted ourselves off.

"Thanks for not giving us away," I said.

"Yeah, you're a good duck, even with that snot rag stuck on your head," Eddy said, grinning at Granny.

My mouth fell open. The scary shopkeeper had effectively saved our necks, and Eddy complimented and insulted her in the same breath.

I grabbed Eddy and backed toward the door, not sure what Granny might do. The heel of my shoe came down on one of the lost crawfish with an unsatisfying, squishy crunch.

I shook my shoe, trying to dislodge the gooey remains.

Granny crossed her arms under her drooping chest. She gave us the evil eye, daring us to make another move. "Fifteen bucks."

"But—"

"Inflation," Granny said.

After coughing up the dough, we skirted the main thoroughfare and made our second bid for freedom. We hustled into the parking lot without further trouble, passing two uniformed cops and a number of security guards who looked like they were on a mission. I hoped they were on the hunt for the two mobsters.

JT and Coop leaned against my pickup with Dawg perched on his haunches between them. As soon as they saw us running toward them, Coop called out, "What's wrong?" Cigarette smoke plumed from his nostrils and he reminded me of a bull exhaling in the icy air of winter.

JT headed for the passenger side. "Are you two okay?"

"Get in!" I yanked the driver's door open. Coop flicked his cigarette to the pavement and scrambled into the back seat. Dawg hopped into the rear with him.

Eddy stopped a few feet behind me, in full brakes-on mode. "What in hell is that beast?"

"Eddy, it's okay, it's Dawg." Don't get stubborn on me now, I prayed. I looked over her shoulder for any sign of Vincent and Pudge.

"That—that monster is your dog?"

I began to sweat. "Come on Eddy, it's okay. He won't hurt you, I promise. You like dogs."

Eddy's tennis shoes didn't budge. "I thought you got one of them poodle dogs, not some—some monstrous mutt!"

This was not the time to debate the relative size of the newest member of our family. After some swift cajoling, we were on the move. Most of Dawg's front end was wedged between JT and me while somehow, Coop, the latter half of Dawg, and Eddy managed to cram into the back seat.

I peeled out onto Lake Street and headed for the freeway, watching for a tail.

JT said, "What in the hell happened back there? And what is that smell?"

A fishy odor wafted through the cab. Apparently I didn't get all the squashed crawfish guts out of the grooves in the bottom of my shoe. Dawg swiped his tongue around his lolling lips. Dead fish was probably a favorite snack.

"Ding and Ling spotted us," Eddy said, excitement still evident in her voice.

"Pudge fell right into the crawfish pond." I said, my words tripping over each other in the after-rush of adrenaline.

"What?" Coop asked.

I said, "We ducked into a fish stand, hid behind one of the display cases—"

"And the snot rag lady—"

"Eddy!" I said.

"I wasn't the one who stuffed a used tissue under glasses I stuck on my forehead instead of on my eyeballs."

I eyed Eddy through the rear-view mirror. "The storekeeper at the fish place used her forehead for an eyeglass holder, and used the bridge of the glasses for stashing her Kleenex. Anyway—"

"She didn't rat us out to Ding and Ling," Eddy finished for me. "Then we snuck out of there and here we are!" Eddy punctuated the end of the tale with a nod and crossed her arms with a satisfied humph. She sat like that for a moment and then leaned forward. "Where are we going?"

"Vincent and Pudge are in the market? Right now?" JT whipped out her cell.

"Yeah, maybe. They were, at any rate." I weaved through a pack of cars.

"Jesus," she said. I could sense her eyes rolling skyward as she punched buttons on her phone. She was soon relaying information to The Powers That Be on the other end of the connection.

"Hope you get those two goof bats," Eddy told JT once she'd hung up. "And hello! Where are we going?"

I said, "We have to get the nuts and spring Rocky."

The blank expression on Eddy's face reminded me we needed to catch her up on the traumatic events of the past day. She sure took being kidnapped in stride. I breathed deep and wished for a double Fuzzy Navel as I launched into it.

"So," Eddy said once we'd concluded. "You found a dead body, stole a dog—"

"Not stole," Coop said. "He followed us."

Eddy waved her hand. "Semantics, child. Now, where was I? The body, the dog. Shay, you impersonated a warehouse inspector, you two stole a truck full of almonds after preying on the kindness of that poker buddy of your father's, and you have a police officer who is sitting right here instead of hauling you both to jail. Gotta love that!" Her smile faded. "And Buzz and Rita have Rocky. Damn."

SIXTEEN

AFTER JT PICKED UP her car from the Denny's parking lot, she followed us the rest of the way to the cabin. She'd shadowed us because she claimed she wanted to be sure we made it okay, especially since Vincent and Pudge were still unaccounted for. I didn't know if it was duty she felt or if she really just didn't trust us and wanted to keep her eye on things.

Everyone piled out and we scattered, JT and me to walk Dawg, Eddy to use the bathroom, and Coop to smoke. Thankfully the truck and container of nuts remained where we'd parked it.

With Dawg on a leash, I wandered away from the house, over scruffy leaf- and twig-laden ground to a pint-sized beach that lay directly in front of the house. JT trudged along behind us. Dawg pulled hard on the leash, no doubt wanting to take a swim. I didn't want to deal with a soggy mongrel, so I kept a tight grip. We came to a stop on wave-rippled sand a few feet away from the water's edge. Dawg got over his momentary pout at not being able to take a dip and nosed around the weeds growing on the bank.

The lake spread out in front of us, maybe half a mile across and a quarter mile wide. Ripples in the water sparkled in the sun.

I said, "JT, what exactly did you mean about working on the bingo situation, and that Kinky was a small fish?"

For a moment I wondered if she'd heard me. She breathed deeply, and then shifted to face me as she exhaled. The sunlight caught subtle, reddish highlights in her dark hair, and her eyes were obsidian. Her face was impassive, but a crease right between her brows implied conflicted emotions.

"I . . . we, I mean Tyrell and I, have been working in conjunction with the FBI for some time on Mafia infiltration in the Twin Cities." Her gaze left my face and fastened on something over my shoulder. "We've been investigating gambling venues for traces of organized crime. We've mostly come up empty except for Stanley Anderson and Pig's Eye Bingo. Mr. Anderson apparently owes—or I suppose I should say, *owed*—a hefty sum to the New Jersey Massioso crime family." She crossed her arms as if warding off a chill. "We think the Family put pressure on Anderson to start laundering some of their dirty money through the bingo operation."

"So you've been, like, casing the barge?"

"We've had our sights on Kinky for over a year. We were about to close down his operation when we realized something more was going on beyond dirty money. Theodore Mahoney—Pudge, to you—and Vincent Ragozzi are hanging onto their Family membership by an extremely thin thread. This nut deal was the last chance to hold onto their status in the Family, and maybe onto their lives."

"But what's the big deal about a load of nuts? Is it the nuts themselves they want or is it the symbolic act of following though on the deal?"

"No idea. But they're absolutely desperate, and that seems to indicate a whole lot more's going on than a simple case of stolen almonds. That's why I hung around the other night. I just knew you all were in trouble—"

"But Coop—"

"Shay, we just wanted to talk to him. Like I told you before, we didn't think he was involved in the murder, but we have to cover all bases. He could have overheard something that didn't seem important but might have broken the case for us. Or not."

I could've kicked myself. If we'd come clean in the first place, none of this might have happened. Stupid, stupid, stupid.

JT put a finger under my chin and forced me to meet her eyes. I did so, reluctantly. "What's done is done. We have to figure out what happens now. This time we have a solid opportunity to nab Pudge and Vincent and round up Buzz and Rita and free your friend."

My mouth went dry and I swallowed hard, struggling for composure on a number of levels. Dawg's rope suddenly jerked and nearly yanked me off my feet, effectively disrupting the emotion of the moment. Dawg fussed and whined as he tried to bully his way toward a huge old maple tree in pursuit of a couple of frisky squirrels.

JT stared at me a moment longer with those dark eyes, then looked away and took a breath.

"You make me crazy," I said, my voice low. Both my hands were now on Dawg's leash.

"Let's not even go there. Jesus. I just can't think when you get too close."

A rakish grin spread across my face, but I remained prudently silent as I took a step away from JT and wondered why that confession pleased me so much.

————

After Dawg had his fill of squirrel chasing (which didn't take more than five minutes since all wildlife fled the vicinity as soon as he lumbered up to the tree), we regrouped in the living room with Eddy and Coop.

Eddy said, "Why you don't get 'em together in some rock pit— isn't that where stuff like that always happens?—and shoot 'em all!" She banged one fist on the coffee table. "'Specially Ding and Ling. Shameful, trussing an old lady up like that."

I suppressed a grin and watched JT's reaction to Eddy's outburst. Her face remained passive, but the twinkle in her eye was unmistakable.

JT said, "Tell me again when you're supposed to turn the truck over to Rita and company."

I checked my watch. "At four this afternoon. It's noon now." I suppressed a yawn and rubbed my eyes. The scant hours of sleep were catching up with me. We'd been running hot on guts and adrenaline and I was just about tapped out. Again. "I'm glad we brought that damn nut truck up here, off everyone's radar. Maybe we can crash for just a little—"

JT's cell rang, interrupting me. She answered it, and as she listened, her face tightened. Eyes that had softened were once again remote. She hung up and said, "Sorry to do this to you, but I have to head back. One of my informants in an unrelated case was just found in an alley, and he's barely alive, so—" She trailed off as she patted her pockets then pulled out her keys.

"Go," I said. "We'll meet up with you and Detective Johnson at two at the Rabbit Hole."

"Okay. You all be very careful." For a brief second, JT locked her gaze on me and then disappeared out the door.

We decided to eat something and heated up some old frozen dinners that were stashed in the freezer while we caught the end of the twelve o'clock news. Pudge and Vincent's antics had not yet hit the airwaves.

My cell vibrated. I set my barely eaten chicken fettuccine on the coffee table and snatched the phone off my belt. The Rabbit Hole phone number flashed on the tiny screen. I stood, flipping it open as I strode into the kitchen in search of something to wash the fettuccine down.

"Shay?" Kate's voice sounded unusually high pitched. "We have a couple of—visitors—here. They, uh, want to talk to you."

My heart rate picked up and the couple bites of fettuccine in my stomach turned to shards of glass. "Who?"

"They didn't give me their names but assured me you'd know who they were." Her voice sounded more constricted by the moment, like she was about to burst into tears. "They have guns. They said they want the goods right now. What goods?" Her voice rose higher. "They said they'd cut off my fingers and once they were done with my hands, if they didn't get what they wanted they'd start on my toes." She made a panicked, strangled sound.

"Oh shit." I paced around the kitchen table, one hand on the top of my head. Pudge and Vincent were pissed and deadly, like a couple of rattlesnakes who had their tails stepped on.

"Where are they right now?"

"Eddy's living room. They closed up the café and now they're drinking lattes they forced me to make." Then she whispered fiercely, but so quietly I could hardly hear, "I hope they choke." Kate was on the brink, but I was relieved to hear she still had some fight in her.

"Let me talk to them." I stopped pacing and grabbed onto the back slat of one of the kitchen chairs for support.

Grumbling sounds bled through the receiver, and then Vincent said, "Listen, bitch. We're through fucking around. We want the nuts and the tape. Now. No, actually sooner than now. Every ten minutes you aren't here with our stuff your sassy little helper loses a finger."

It would take at least forty-five minutes on a good day with no traffic to get to the Rabbit Hole, probably closer to an hour. At that rate, Kate would be missing all the slim appendages off one hand and they'd be starting in on the other.

Play for time. "I'm at least an hour and a half away."

I heard a sharp intake of air and then a disgusted sigh. "Christ. You got an hour. Then little Miss Barista here'll be whipping up those fancy drinks single-handed. And if we see any cops, she's dead. Dead with a capital D!" Vincent roared the last part into the receiver. I heard Kate scream, and then he disconnected, leaving me staring at my phone. With great effort I suppressed a sudden urge to slam it against the wall.

SEVENTEEN

"Drive," Eddy said. The tires hummed as we streaked down Interstate 35. She kept a hawk eye on Dawg, afraid she might be attacked by the vicious canine. Coop rumbled along behind us at a slower clip in the semi with the almonds. I tried multiple times to call JT on her cell, but she didn't pick up. Vincent's prior warning about cops still echoed through my head, and I didn't dare try to alert anyone else.

I said, "What if Kate—"

"Don't even think it, Shay. She's going to be fine."

"But—"

Eddy leveled her eyes at me. "Shay ..." The warning in her voice was clear.

On the mutt front, Eddy was slowly caving in. Dawg managed to lay his head on her shoulder. Eddy's hand rested on top of his neck. It wasn't moving yet, but I gave her about two more minutes.

We passed the ramp for 694 and zoomed toward 94. 12:40. We'd be at the Hole in another fifteen minutes. With a little more luck, all of Kate's fingers would still be attached.

At five minutes to one, we rolled off 94 to the Hennepin/Lyndale exit and on to Hennepin Avenue, cut down some side streets, and slowly passed the Rabbit Hole. The lights were off and the CLOSED sign hung in the window.

I turned the corner at the end of the block, parked, and pressed my back against the seat, holding tight to the steering wheel.

Dawg was now wedged between me and Eddy, his head in her lap, and she was smoothing the fur between his eyes with one hand while the other stroked the silky, loose lip that was draped across her thigh. She was a goner.

Unable to sit still, I got out of my seat to pace. Outside of the truck, a wave of impending doom left me breathless. I gasped and said, "I think I should go in. Now."

"No way." Eddy could cut a person in two with her glare. "We wait for Coop. We stick to the plan." We'd hastily concocted what I knew was an absolutely lame-brained plot that involved first Coop and I going into the Rabbit Hole, and then Eddy following a couple of minutes later, making as big a racket as she could. The idea was to distract the bad boys and get Kate out of there. How we were really going to pull it off, I had no idea. But we had to do something.

I gazed at the ground and nudged a loose rock with my foot. My heartbeat thudded triple-time to the second hand on my watch as we waited for Coop.

Eddy had finally decided Dawg was no more a threat than peanut butter. She kneeled on the sidewalk vigorously rubbing the belly he displayed for attention.

"Told you he was okay," I said.

Eddy gave me another pointed glare. "Much better than some of the other strays that you bring home." Eddy said. "Now that JT, she's okay. For a stray."

I blushed.

After an interminable wait, Coop chugged past us, parked the truck a couple of blocks away in the lot of an old church, and hoofed it back to where we waited.

"Looks like you two made up," Coop said as he looked down at Dawg, stretched out at Eddy's feet. Actually, he was lying on top of her feet.

"All right," I said. "Focus. Remember the plan. Coop and I go into the Hole. We leave the front door unlocked. Eddy, you wait three minutes, call 911, and then come in, make a big racket, yell that the cops are on the way or something. Once you distract Pudge and Vincent, Coop, you get Kate out the back, if you can. I'll help Eddy out with the cleanup," I finished with more confidence than I felt. "And then, hopefully, the cops will be there."

Coop handed his cell phone to Eddy and we synchronized watches.

Eddy said, "Wish I had my Whacker. This is just about too *Law & Order* for me."

I felt like I was floating in the trees above, watching a scene in a movie play out before my very eyes. I understood there was risk in doing this, but after what these idiots did to Eddy and now to Kate, I wanted their heads maybe more than JT and Tyrell did. I purposely tried not to think about what could happen to Kate, Coop, Eddy, and me if things went south. Or how furious Detective Bordeaux—and the Minneapolis Police Department and the FBI—were going to be.

Dawg rolled to his feet and chuffed, a deep furrow creasing his brow. He was a sensitive mutt, somehow attuned to the emotions around him. I crouched down and wrapped my arms around his neck, and he pressed his heavy jowls into my shoulder. He gave me a final swipe of his tongue. I coaxed him into the pickup, and he hung his head through the half-open window. His eyebrows were raised expectantly, as if he thought we should get going already. Our last time-out was over. Game on.

———

Our footsteps echoed in tandem on the cracked sidewalk as Coop and I neared the front door of the Rabbit Hole. As we closed in, he leaned down and whispered, "I'm sorry I got you and Eddy and Kate into this mess."

"You know I'd do anything to help you, and I know you'd do the same for me."

He draped an arm over my shoulders. Not for the first time, I thought that one day he was going to make some woman very happy.

I dug in the pocket of my jeans and my fingers wrapped around the familiar outline of the key ring. Reflection from the sun made it hard to see in the windows. I slid the key home, unlocked the door, and pushed it open. The bells banging against the glass clanged ominously.

The tables were all intact, the chairs tucked beneath them. A cozy fire burned in the fireplace, at odds with the situation. Coop followed me inside and shut the door. I scanned the unmanned counter with a pang. What was proper protocol when calling on kidnappers?

Coop yelled, "Hey! It's Nick Cooper and Shay O'Hanlon."

We stood in the middle of the café waiting for a response, surrounded by the unsettling yet comforting and familiar aroma of the shop. I felt like a stranger in my own place, a foreigner in my own home. Seconds ticked by like minutes. A low voice finally growled, "How about that. You're early. Turn around toward the window and put your hands over your heads." Vincent. He was close. It took me a moment to see he was sitting in one of the chairs by the fireplace, mostly hidden in shadow. It didn't take nearly as long to realize that a handgun was pointed in our direction.

We raised our arms in tandem and slowly pivoted toward the picture window.

Leather creaked as Vincent rose from the chair and the sound of his footsteps was loud on the hard floor as he walked up behind us. My mouth was parched and my chest tightened, making it hard to breathe.

"Do you have what I want?" It felt like he was breathing down the back of my neck.

"I think so," Coop told him.

"You think so. You're a funny guy, aren't you? Where's the tape?"

I said, "In the side pocket of my pants." Vincent slid a hand down the outside of my right leg. I tried not to cringe at his touch. "No, the other one."

He moved over to my left leg and tugged the videocassette from my cargo pocket. "Ah, yes. You've passed the first part of the test. Now what about my nuts?"

"We're not telling you that until you let Kate go," I responded, proud that my voice only quavered a little. "Where is she?"

Silence reigned a moment longer. "Keep your hands on your heads and walk backward. I'll tell you when to stop. One move I don't like and I'll shoot a hole in the back of your kneecaps. Got it?"

We shuffled awkwardly backward following the sound of Vincent's voice. I wanted to sneak a peek at my watch and see how much of the three minutes had expired before Eddy showed up, but I didn't have the guts.

Vincent guided us through the café, past the French doors, and into Eddy's living room. "Okay, now you can turn around. Very slowly." Coop and I complied.

On the couch sat a very pissed off Kate, apparently unharmed. Her hands were bound in front of her with white clothesline rope, and all her fingers appeared to be intact. Scowling and red-faced, she glared back and forth between Pudge and Vincent. She might be tiny, but she had a strong constitution. I wanted to either cry or shout in relief.

Pudge perched on Eddy's coffee table. He held a dull, black semi-automatic gun on Kate. Eddy was going to be one knotted Knitter when she heard her precious crafting glossies had been violated by the gangster's sizable ass. However, she'd be happy to see he had a hell of a robin's egg on one side of his head, laced with a jagged cut that had scabbed up in clotted bumps, and the beginnings of a beautiful shiner.

"You okay?" I asked Kate, and made a move to step toward her.

"Don't." Vincent barked. "Stay right there."

I froze in place as Kate glared at Vincent. She said between gritted teeth, "They owe us for two lattes, a biscotti, and a piece of lemon cheesecake."

"Christ," Pudge muttered, "everyone wants a piece."

Vincent nudged me in the shoulder with his gun. "So there she is. Where's my fucking nuts?"

"We said we'd tell you that when you let her go," Coop said. "As in, after she walks out the door."

Before Vincent or Pudge could reply, the bells on the front door chimed. Eddy's voice floated to us loud and clear. Her singing was garbled but the words sounded familiar.

Pudge stood abruptly. "What the—" Eddy's magazines cascaded to the floor in a heap.

Like lightning, Vincent thwacked me in the back of the head with an open palm, hard enough to snap my head forward. I yelped as Vincent hissed, "Didn't you lock the goddamn door when you came in?"

I rubbed the back of my head. "You didn't tell me to do that."

"Jesus Christ. Sit your asses down." Vincent motioned at the couch with his gun.

I sat next to Kate, with Coop on her other side.

Weird and *bizarre* couldn't begin to describe what was happening. I suddenly realized Eddy was belting out Pat Benatar's "Hit Me with Your Best Shot" at the top of her lungs. Completely out of tune. I didn't think she even knew who Pat Benatar was. I fought to bite back hysterical laughter.

Vincent made a guttural sound in the back of his flabby throat. "Pudge, keep an eye on these jokers. I'll go out and deal with this." He hitched up his pants with one hand and stomped toward the door, gun in his other beefy hand, hidden behind his back.

Pudge followed Vincent to the double French doors and positioned his rotund body mostly out of view of the front of the shop. His head bobbed right and left between us and the café, like some kind of deranged pelican on crack.

Vincent said, loud enough to be heard above the screeching, "Well, if it ain't the old bat."

Eddy ended her completely slaughtered karaoke attempt and said, "Mouthta fobo dimdum simsum."

Vincent boomed, "What the hell—"

Eddy drowned him out with another flood of mishmashed words. Kudos for creativity.

Pudge's attention was focused on the commotion out front, I caught Kate's eye and jerked my head toward the kitchen. She nodded and gathered herself to rise, but Pudge shot a glance our way. She froze. Then he zoned back in on the confrontation between Vincent and Eddy.

Vincent said, "Shut up! I'm telling you—"

Eddy screeched like a hen in heat. In the most bizarre voice, totally unrecognizable, she said, "How dare you kidnap an innocent dame!" She reverted to spewing out more insanity. If I didn't know her better, I'd have sworn she was loony tunes.

Praying that Pudge didn't look back, I mouthed, one, two, three. Kate jumped up from the couch like a popped cork and zoomed out of the room. Pudge didn't even notice. His hand had gradually relaxed, and now he held the gun almost casually at his side.

Eddy continued with her only semi-comprehensible tirade.

Vincent said, "Listen, you old hag—"

"Don't you call me an old hag, you nasty 'napper." Eddy must have had enough. "No one messes with Edwina Quartermaine and gets away with it! How do you like this?" There was a muffled clunk.

Vincent yowled. "That was my shin, you bitch!"

Oh shit. The woman was going to get herself shot.

I nudged Coop and motioned toward Pudge. My gaze settled on a heavy book lying on an end table beside the couch. It was *A History of Crocheting and Knitting around the World*. I'd bought the book at the indie-feminist bookstore, True Colors, for Eddy last Christmas. The tome had to weigh ten pounds. Holding my breath, I picked up the book and gripped it tight.

Pudge was now completely absorbed in the argument in the other room. I mouthed to Coop, "Ready?"

He nodded.

I exploded up from my seat. In two long strides, I was across the carpet. I swung the heavy book with all my might and felt horrifying, primal joy surge through me as it whammed into the back of Pudge's skull. His forehead smashed against the doorjamb with a sickening thud. He slithered down the doorframe like a cartoon character. I dropped the book and wrested the gun from his limp fingers.

Coop and I stampeded through the French doors. Vincent stood in the middle of the café, sighting down the barrel of his gun at Eddy. She was near the front door, holding up a chair, lion-tamer style. Vincent glanced our way. In slow motion, he swung the gun toward us.

A freight train roared in my ears. I forgot the gun in my own hand and had no idea where Coop was. I blindly charged Vincent. His mouth opened, and I saw his eyes widen a fraction of a second before I hit him with a tackle that Chicago Bear "The Fridge" Perry would have been proud of. Vincent's gun flew from his grasp in an arc that seemed slow and graceful. I didn't hear it hit the floor. Didn't hear anything but the cacophony in my head. My vision was muted and fuzzy around the edges. All I could focus on was a tunnel filled with the body of an evil thug.

We hit the polished wood of the Rabbit Hole floor hard. I landed heavily on top of Vincent, and I heard air whoosh out. I tried to knee him but caught his thigh instead. He grunted. One of his hands grabbed under my chin, squeezing my windpipe. I tried to suck in a breath, no luck. I took a wild swing at his head with my gun hand. I barely registered the fact I still had the weapon. Vincent let go of my neck and brought up his hands to block the blow just before I clipped his nose. He grabbed my hand and we struggled for the gun.

I frantically grappled with him, panicked to keep control of the gun. I tried to head-butt him but couldn't manage enough force to get past our arms. Tied up in a deadly tug-of-war, I vaguely registered a growling noise. Was I making that ghastly sound, or was it coming from Vincent?

The metal edges of the gun felt knife-sharp against my palm as he desperately tried to pry it from my grasp. Then there was a violent explosion. The gun jerked hard in my fist, recoil traveling up my arm to my shoulder like lightning.

I shifted right, off-balance. Vincent bucked and rolled out from under me. I fell to my side.

It took a moment to realize he wasn't coming at me again. He was curled in a fetal position screaming. Mutely, I scrambled backward as the fuzzy room reconstituted itself and once again became the familiar Rabbit Hole.

Despite a strange sucking sound in my ears, suddenly I could hear. I used a table to boost myself off the floor.

Vincent shouted, "—SHOT MY PINKIE OFF, YOU CRAZY BITCH! YOU, YOU …" He trailed off in a wail.

I looked at the gun miraculously still in my hand as Vincent howled. I caught motion out of the corner of my eye, and saw that Eddy stood over Vincent with her chair raised.

She said, "Come on, you big oaf, give me a reason to give you another lump."

"SHE BLEW MY FUCKING FINGER OFF!"

Coop stood near the French doorway, his eyes wild. "Shit oh shit oh shit. You okay, Shay?" He held Vincent's gun on Pudge, who sat slumped unresisting on the floor, awake but dazed, blood running down the side of his face.

"Jesus," I croaked. "What—"

"Shay, you're not shot, right?" he asked.

"No, no, I don't think …" I gasped for air and looked at my midsection and legs, saw one knee covered with a dark, sticky substance. My stomach bottomed out until I touched the goo and realized it wasn't blood. I gingerly sniffed then licked my finger.

Thank God, I'd just rolled through a particularly gummy caramel mocha latte spill. "No, I'm okay."

"Holy shit, little Miss Tenacious Protector," Coop said, his gaze locked on Pudge, "He could've killed you!"

"But he didn't." I said. Suddenly my legs went noodly. I slid into a chair, panting and light-headed.

JT, Tyrell, and what looked like an entire SWAT team chose that moment to barge in the front door, and more chaos descended upon the coffee shop.

———

By quarter after one, the semi-conscious Pudge and a bandaged Vincent were in the capable hands of the authorities. Eddy, Coop, Kate, Dawg, and I crowded in Eddy's kitchen and sipped Eddy's hot chocolate.

JT and Tyrell made a brief appearance after they hauled out Vincent and Pudge and told us to wait for them. I figured under normal circumstances, we'd be whisked down to the station to make official statements. The crime scene folks had already swabbed my hand for gunpowder residue and confiscated Vincent's gun. I suspected that JT and Tyrell were doing everything they could to keep us out of after-arrest red tape so they could coordinate our next step.

Dawg made quick work of Kate, who was all over him, rubbing and smooching and patting his wiggling body. As she sat at the table, Dawg nosed at her lap, trying to keep her hands on his head. He scooted over to Coop for attention and continued around the table, lavishing adoration on all of us. I doubted he'd ever felt this much love in his entire life.

Kate said, "I knew something big was going on." She fixed me with her trademark I-told-you-so glare. "Now you can't be mad at me for talking to JT."

"As usual, you're right. I don't know why I bother to argue." My grin belied the tone of my voice, and I sat back, still feeling thick-headed.

Eddy was relating to Kate every moment of her time in captivity when my cell chirped. The caller ID displayed no number. I stepped outside, quietly shutting the screen door behind me, feeling once again like I was stuck in *Groundhog Day*.

"Hello?"

The cultured voice on the other end immediately raised the hackles on the back of my neck. "The timeline's moved up. We want the nuts and the dog now."

"Now? But—"

"No buts. You bring what we want and you'll get what you want."

My mind raced. The Rocky Rescue Plan had hardly been discussed. Coop, Eddy, and I had only the ability to concentrate on the present emergency, and now I realized we were in for more problems yet.

"We need more time—"

Rita butted in, unbecoming edginess pitching her voice up a number of octaves. "Maybe this will clear things up for you." The sound became muffled, like a palm had covered the receiver. I listened but couldn't quite make out the brief, jumbled conversation.

Then, "Shay O'Hanlon, ohhh—" the choking sound of a swallowed sob burst through the phone. I'd lost count of the times my heart had stopped in the last twenty-four hours.

Rocky's voice quavered and he hiccupped. "Shay O'Hanlon, they hurt me so bad, Shay!"

The familiar backyard, the sounds of singing birds, and the whitish-yellow rays of the sun beaming down through leafless branches faded from my awareness, and all I could hear was Rocky's yip of pain in my ear.

A quick intake of breath came from the other end of the line and then a loud, "Owie!"

"Rocky!" I said. "Rocky—"

"Please, please make them stop hurting me. I don't like Miss Rita very much anymore, Shay O'Hanlon. Owwwww."

"Rocky, I'm—"

"Please Shay O'Hanlon, it hurts bad. They said no police officers, Shay O'Hanlon—"

Buzz cut Rocky off. "Listen here, O'Hanlon. I want that truck, and I want my damn mutt. And I want 'em now," he bellowed in my ear. "Go to that closed gas station next to Grizzly. Park behind the building. You don't show, and Rita's gonna do a whole lot more than make snot run from the little crybaby."

The line disconnected on another yelp from Rocky. I snapped my phone shut and bent over at the waist, chest heaving. Fighting not to throw up, I tried to gain some control over my body. I wondered how much a person would take before they cracked up, broke down, or did both. Panic swirled through my brain.

What to do? I tried to hold my Protector instincts in check, but hearing Rocky's cries brought out both fury and terror.

"Fuck," I muttered and stood straight, forcing myself to breathe slow and deep. The nausea subsided somewhat, replaced by full-body shakes. I clipped my phone into its holster on the second attempt and clenched my fists tight. I needed a plan. I had to get Coop and Dawg away from Kate and Eddy without arousing suspicion. Then we had to figure out how to handle this. If I could only get to JT without alerting every cop around, I could explain the latest developments to her.

I jogged around the house and peered through the plate glass in the Rabbit Hole. Detective Johnson was in deep conversation with a couple of guys wearing black suits, and no one looked like they would take kindly to interruption. Four squads were parked in front of the Hole, and a cluster of uniformed cops were engrossed in conversation on the sidewalk.

JT was across the road talking to a man in a white oxford shirt, sleeves rolled halfway up his forearms. He leaned into her space, his finger jabbing the air forcefully as he spoke. The look on her face alternated between sheepish and defensive. His lips stopped moving and JT started to say something. Then he was back in her face again. I could only assume she was getting a royal ass chewing for not following proper procedure or some other cop infraction.

I could march up to them and ask to talk to JT and in the process piss off her boss even more, or I could try calling her on my cell once we were on the way. The cell phone idea won. I slunk from the front of the house and ran around the building to the kitchen. I paused at the screen door, watching Eddy bang the table with her fist. Kate's eyebrows shot up in surprise, and then her forehead wrinkled as she followed the ins and outs of Eddy's tale. I felt a twinge at the unfairness of my plight. I wanted to be as oblivious as they were.

With a whispered prayer, I yanked the door open and stepped inside. Coop was leaning back in his chair, one long leg crossed over his knee, a half-grin shadowing his face as he listened to Eddy embellish her story. I caught his eye, and gave a slight jerk of my head toward the door. The front legs of his chair met the floor with a soft thunk and he stood.

I said quietly, "Coop, let's walk Dawg while Eddy finishes telling Kate what happened."

At the mention of his name, Dawg bounced to his enormous feet from an old comforter Eddy had laid out for him. His sizeable rear wiggled back and forth at the sound of the word *walk,* and he skittered over and pushed his body against me in thrilled anticipation. I put my hand on the top of his head, relieved to see my trembling had subsided.

Eddy shot a look at me and then quickly returned her attention to Kate without missing a beat. This version of events had grown epic in proportion compared to the tale we'd heard earlier, and I'd have poked fun at Eddy under normal circumstances.

I called over my shoulder as the screen door slammed shut, "We'll be back in a bit."

Kate waved, too enthralled with Eddy's growing-taller-by-the-second tale to pay much attention.

Coop had one hand wrapped around Dawg's rope. I grabbed his other hand and dragged him past the garage and into the alley. "Coop," I whispered urgently. "Come on!"

"What?" He was being yanked in half as Dawg pulled him one way and I jerked him another.

"Things have changed—Buzz and Rita want the nuts and Dawg now."

"But—"

"Now," I repeated. "Where's the truck?"

We sped along the alley, Dawg trotting to keep up.

"It's a couple of blocks over."

"You have the keys, right?"

"Yeah … what happened?"

I rapidly filled him in about my phone call.

"Holy shit. But don't you think that JT—"

"I already tried to talk to her. She was getting a serious reaming from her boss, and Johnson was busy inside with the men in black. I don't want to get either of them in more hot water."

"Isn't that what cops are for? To get people out of hot water?"

I hadn't thought about it that way. But I'd already burned up too much time as it was. "We need to go. I'll call her once we're on the way, okay?"

"Okay. Fine."

I hazarded a look at Coop as we hurried along the cracked asphalt. His head was down, and his shaggy hair swung against his face, obscuring his eyes. He peered sideways at me, through the fine strands. "How are we going to get out of this mess?"

The truck was in sight now. I picked up the pace. Even Coop, with his long legs, had to step it up.

"Haven't got that figured out yet."

"I need to show you something. Here." Coop handed me Dawg's rope. He reached into his front pocket and pulled out a gun. Pudge's gun.

I stopped dead. "What are you doing with that?"

"The cops busted in and I freaked. With my record, I was afraid…" He trailed off and shrugged. "I stuck it in my pocket."

"God, Coop, you should've—oh hell, never mind. Too freaking late now. Maybe it'll come in handy."

"You take it. I can't believe I touched that instrument of death." Coop gingerly handed me the weapon. It wasn't much bigger than the palm of my hand. Not much we could do about it at this point, so I looked furtively around and slid it into the side cargo pocket of my pants. We resumed walking. The gun banged into my knee every time I took a step.

"I was scared," Coop said. "Stupid, I know."

"Maybe it'll be the great equalizer."

"Or a spike in the coffin."

———

The inside of the semi's cab was dirty and grease-stained, well-used. The cloying odor of stale cigarette smoke and gasoline swirled through the vehicle, making me dizzy.

Dawg perched on the seat between Coop and me, his lip hooked on an incisor, grimacing in as much distaste at his surroundings as we were. Coop sucked hard on a cigarette, keeping it close to his open window, and the smell was almost better than the stale odors that had long ago seeped into the upholstery and headliner.

Sharp metal dug into the soft skin on the side of my knee as Coop wheeled around a corner and rolled down a ramp onto southbound 35W. I gingerly pulled out the weapon and set it on the cracked vinyl seat beside me, careful to keep it away from Dawg's paws.

My movements caught Coop's attention. "What in the hell are you doing with that thing?"

I eyed the gun for a moment. "Not sure."

Coop looked back at the road. "Put it away! You're going to get us killed."

"That's what I'm trying *not* to do."

Dawg's head swung from me to Coop, and then he returned his worried gaze my direction. He settled down next to Coop with a deep sigh, resting his head on Coop's leg.

"So," Coop said as he changed lanes and navigated the new maze of ramps of the 35W/Crosstown commons. "How are we gonna play this out?"

Only fifteen minutes had passed since Rita's call, but it felt like hours. "They want to meet in that lot by the gas station."

"The one where we parked after George left?"

"Yeah. I suppose they want the truck close to the terminal, but not so close that attention is drawn to the situation if there's a showdown." I eyed the gun again and felt a throb of pain in my temple. I focused out the windshield on the car in front of us. It had bumper stickers all over its rear end, but the vehicle was too far away for me to make out what they said. I rubbed my forehead in a vain attempt to calm the thumping that had set in.

"Okay, how about this," Coop said as he checked my side mirror and shifted lanes. We were now heading east on 494, away from downtown. "We'll hand this jalopy over to them, get Rocky, and get the hell out."

I sat silently for a minute. "What about Dawg?"

"What about Dawg?"

"I can't give him back, Coop. Buzz'll kill him."

Coop chewed on the inside of his cheek. "I wonder why Buzz wants the mutt back so bad?"

We both contemplated Dawg's chances with Buzz. I said, "Maybe because he's a redneck who can't stand for someone to have something that belongs to him." I ran a finger over the ridge above Dawg's eye. "This time the redneck goes empty-handed."

"I'm with you." He held his fist out to me and I knocked it with my own.

"Let's play it out and go with the flow. It's more or less worked for us so far."

"Sounds like a plan to me. Call JT."

JT didn't answer, but I left a message and hoped she'd get it soon. I wondered if she was still in the midst of her verbal lashing.

The rest of the ride was uneventful. I knew that as soon as JT found out we'd bailed, there'd be hell to pay, even if I had left her a message. I hoped when this was all over, she'd understand why we took off—provided Coop, Rocky, and I came out of this un-harmed.

As the road whizzed by, I thought about my feelings for JT. It'd been a long time since I'd had interest beyond the physical in any-one. I wondered if what I was feeling for her was simply a result of the overly charged emotions that came with life, death, and feloni-ous break-ins.

My musings ended when Coop pulled off the freeway and headed down 61 toward the Grizzly Terminal. After a few minutes, the gas station came into view, and although I couldn't see it, the entrance to the shipping terminal was only a quarter-mile away.

I opened my cell, found Rita's number, and hit redial. For an instant I was afraid she wasn't going to pick up. She did.

"We're here," I said without preamble.

"What about the dog?" The sound of Rita's voice grated on my last nerve.

My throat constricted, but I said, "He's here, too."

"Park around behind the building and get out of the truck. Stand in front of it and wait." She disconnected.

"Go to the back of the station," I directed Coop. As he slowly eased into the parking lot, I scanned the area for Buzz and Rita. We came to a rumbling stop behind the station, and I wondered where they were.

Coop killed the engine. "Ready?"

"No."

Neither of us made a move to get out of the cab.

"Do you know how to use a gun?" I asked Coop.

"Are you kidding?" He frowned at me. "I save things, not kill them. The Green Beans would revoke my membership."

"Just checking." I picked the weapon up. The metal was cold in my hands, and it felt very final. I didn't know what else to do with it, so I stuck it in my pants at the small of my back. I had a sudden, frightening vision of it accidentally going off and putting a large hole in one of my butt cheeks.

I looked at Coop. "I love you, you fool. Thank you for being my best friend."

He eyed me a moment, then reached over and tousled my hair. "I love you, too."

I caught his hand and pressed it to my cheek, then let it go and opened the door, feeling like we were playing out the disastrous last moments of *Butch Cassidy and the Sundance Kid*.

EIGHTEEN

We climbed out of the semi at the same time, and I coaxed Dawg down once my feet were on the ground. Rita and company weren't in sight, but I felt eyes burning into us from every direction.

Dawg and I met Coop in front of the truck's massive grille. Stillness pressed down, and the only sound was our shuffling feet on the loose gravel. After a couple of tense minutes, a black Lexus pulled in. It rolled to a stop twenty yards away.

The driver's door swung slowly open, and a man who could only be Buzz stepped out onto the dusty ground. He was almost six feet tall, with a solid beer belly and an unruly shock of sparse, mouse-brown hair on the top of his head. A thick, ugly moustache sprouted beneath a bulbous nose, and light-colored whiskers covered his cheeks. His facial hair and Rita's mole-sprouts could really create some hair- and complexion-challenged brats. Ugh.

Buzz wore a faded black t-shirt beneath an unbuttoned, armless green flannel shirt. His Wranglers were held up by a brown belt with a shiny oversized metal buckle that was almost hidden by his overhanging paunch.

He shut the door and stepped forward. Dawg whimpered, cowering between Coop and me. The hard metal of the gun pressed insistently against my back. A drop of nervous sweat slowly trickled down my spine.

Buzz stopped about ten feet away. "Give me the keys and the dog."

"Where's Rocky?" I said.

Buzz glared at me. He swiped a hand over his face and yelled, "Rita!"

A moment later the passenger door popped opened and Rita emerged. Dressed in an expensive, light gray pantsuit she held herself regally despite the desolate surroundings. What did she see in white trash Buzz?

"Get the retard," Buzz said to her.

Rita opened the rear door and reached inside, bringing Rocky out by the ear as if he were a misbehaving ten-year-old.

"Ow, ow, ow." Rocky's voice was hoarse and pain-filled.

Coop stiffened, and I slid my hand slowly behind my back, fingers wrapping around the grip of the gun. Rita dragged Rocky by his ear over to Buzz. Rocky's head was tilted sideways and tear tracks slowly made their way down his cheeks. "Here's the crybaby. Now give Buzz the damn keys," Rita said, the mole on her chin quivering.

Buzz took a step closer and would have taken another, but Dawg growled low in his throat. Buzz stopped and glared at the dog. "You fucking mutt. You'll get yours." His weasly eyes shifted between Coop and me. "You stole my damn dog."

Coop bristled. "We didn't steal him. He escaped from your abusive bullshit, asshole."

"Why you—" Buzz cocked his arm and his hand curled into a fist. He made a move to step closer but halted mid-stride as Dawg stood, hackles raised, his growl louder this time, higher pitched, and his long teeth bared.

Rita still held onto Rocky's ear for dear life, and Rocky's golden eyes were saucers, his face pale.

"Let Rocky go, Rita," I commanded.

"Give Buzz the keys," she countered.

"Let him go," Coop said.

Dawg was still growling low in his throat and kept his eyes zeroed in on Buzz, daring him to make another move.

"Fine." She let go of Rocky's ear and shoved him forward. He stumbled and fell heavily to one knee before he regained his feet and stood, dazed.

"Rocky, walk over to the building and go around to the front," I said. I wanted him as far away from the Showdown at Forlorn Station as he could get. Rocky blinked slowly at me, and then turned toward the structure and wobbled off on unsteady legs.

I redirected my attention to the two monsters before us. Rita sidled over next to Buzz. Both of them uneasily eyed Dawg, whose eyes flicked between the two of them as if he didn't know who the worse threat was.

"Okay, he's free. Give me the damn keys." Buzz narrowed his eyes, pulled a revolver from beneath his flannel shirt tail, and leveled it at us.

My hand was still behind my back, and I tried to tug the gun from my waistband. The air felt weighted, like we were breathing pudding. Beside me, Coop tensed, sensing I was in the midst of doing something but not knowing what.

"Give me the goddamned keys," Buzz roared, and took a long step toward us. As the barrel of the gun cleared my pants, Dawg launched himself at Buzz with a frenzied growl. In one bound, he was upon him and clamped onto Buzz's crotch. An inhuman scream issued from the big man as Dawg's momentum knocked him on his ass. The gun flew from his hand and skittered away, coming to a stop near Rita.

Buzz continued to scream, and Dawg didn't appear to be letting up.

I brought my own gun in front of me but didn't know if I should point it at Rita or Buzz. While I tried to make up my mind, Rita scrambled for Buzz's gun. Coop dove for it at the same time.

Dust kicked up in clouds. Rita and Coop wrestled in the gravel, each trying desperately to get a hold of the weapon.

Suddenly a deafening blast ripped the air, and Coop was propelled violently backward. He landed flat on his back, limbs askew. A large stain appeared on his right shoulder, blood quickly soaking his shirt.

My horrified gaze snapped back to Rita, who scrambled to her feet. She waved the gun around, shell-shocked. Her neatly coiffed black hair was askew, her eyes wild.

She managed to get both hands on the gun and swing it in my direction. The gun in her hand bobbled as her hands shook, but the weapon in mine was rock-steady. My brain ceased processing. It was stuck in a never-ending loop of Coop's name. Rita and I were at an impasse.

"You … you're ruining everything," she spat at me. It was hard to hear over Buzz's howls of pain.

"Drop the gun, Rita," I shouted at her.

She regarded me with eyes so full of anger that I'd have stepped back from the sheer force of her glare if I didn't have a gun pointed at her.

"How could you do this to me?" She glared at Buzz in disgust as he writhed, trying in vain to get away from the vise of Dawg's jaws. I had to hand it to the mutt, he had tenacity. Payback for years of hurt Buzz had heaped on him.

"Drop the gun," I told her again.

Her gaze slid back to me. "You little bitch. You've wrecked it all." Her hands steadied, the gun's barrel pointed square at the center of my chest. My mind screamed at me to shoot while my finger remained frozen on the trigger, unable to squeeze it hard enough to fire.

Before I had a chance to say another word, an object rocketed from somewhere behind me. It struck Rita smack-dab between the eyes. She went down as if the ground had been yanked from beneath her feet.

I blinked once. Then, as if snapping out of a trance, I frantically looked for the source of the damage. Rocky bounced toward me from the side of the truck, surprise and joy spread across his face. "I thwacked her, Shay O'Hanlon! I thwacked her with a rock right in the thinker!"

The little man launched himself at me and I barely had enough time to stuff the gun into a pocket before he wrapped his arms around me. "I did it, Shay O'Hanlon, I did it!"

I squeezed him tight with one arm, frantically grabbing at my cell with the other and dialing 911 as I hobbled both of us over to Coop's crumpled form.

NINETEEN

THE NEXT DAY, FLOWERS and non-latex balloons dotted Coop's dreary white hospital room with a myriad of cheerful colors. Get-well-soon cards lined the edge of the window. It was amazing how much stuff accumulated in the short span of two days.

The other half of the room was unoccupied at the moment. Coop sat, pillows propping him up. A white bandage covered his shoulder. He'd really lucked out. The bullet passed through flesh, missing bone and major arteries. He was facing a painful rehab but would fully recover.

I was settled on the bed opposite Coop's when someone knocked on the door. It slowly swung open, and JT popped her head in, then entered with Tyrell in tow.

"There's the great detecting duo," Coop said.

JT sat down next to me while Tyrell stood at the foot of Coop's bed, his arms crossed.

"I suppose you want details," JT said.

I gave her a no-duh gaze.

"Buzz is out of surgery, and it looks like he's going to emerge with his nuts intact."

I wasn't sure if that was a good thing or a bad thing.

"Rita has a slight concussion but is recovering nicely in a jail cell," she continued. "Rocky has a hell of an arm, not to mention great aim."

Tyrell rumbled, "Rita spilled the beans on what she and Buzz had cooked up. They set Kinky up and stole the nuts after Kinky defaulted on some money he owed Buzz."

"From gambling," JT added. Her shoulder was pressed solidly into mine, and the heat of her skin burned through my t-shirt. It was hard to concentrate on what was being said.

"Buzz was coordinating the shipment and sale of the almonds to thieves down south," Tyrell said. "They would have gotten between two hundred grand and half a mil for the load."

Coop whistled though his teeth. "Damn."

JT said, "Rita planned the whole thing. She overheard Kinky talking to Vincent on the phone about the nuts. She was broke. Squandered all her money gambling. She took out a $350,000 life insurance policy on the hubby, and with the money from the sale of the nuts and the dough from the policy, she was headed back home to Portugal, where she planned on living the high life on the low down."

"I can't believe she was going to take Buzz with her. He wasn't her type at all," I said, acutely aware of every move JT made next to me.

"No, he wasn't," Tyrell said. "But he was her type in that he'd do whatever dirty work she asked of him, including taking out her husband."

Coop said, "So he did kill Luther."

"Yup. Poor guy. Didn't figure out where his money had gone until it was too late. Rita cleaned him out of everything, including his life." JT shook her head.

"And what about Vincent and Pudge?" I asked.

"That was the kicker," Tyrell said. "Both Vincent and Pudge were on the cusp of being taken out by their own mob Family. They'd screwed up one too many operations, and this was their do-it-or-die job. They're the ones who had the almonds stolen in California and brought them here with over a million bucks worth of cocaine hidden in the middle of the load."

My mouth fell.

"What?" Coop said.

JT couldn't wipe the smirk off her face. "Yup. Rita and Buzz had no idea what kind of gold mine they almost hooked."

"Holy cow," Coop said. "No wonder Pudge and Vincent were so desperate to get that truck back. This brings us almost full circle back to Kinky. Did Pudge do him after all?"

JT said, "We got your back-up tape in the mail this morning. Good thinking, making a copy."

"That was all Coop. All I did was seal the envelope shut. It's a good thing we had extra VCRs up at the cabin."

Tyrell chuckled, the sound rolling from deep in his chest. "The video is clear enough to finger Pudge for the murder. Turns out Kinky did pinch his butt, and that insulted Pudge's manliness. He grabbed the first thing at hand and hauled off and walloped Kinky. He didn't intend to kill him, but he's never been known for control."

"What happens now?" I asked.

"Rita and Buzz will hopefully do significant jail time," JT said. "We think Vincent will turn state's evidence against his boss, and Pudge will do whatever Vincent does."

"Damn," Coop muttered.

"So—" I was interrupted by another quick knock on the door, and in breezed Eddy and Rocky.

"Nick Coop, you are okay!" Rocky shuffled up to the edge of the bed, a big smile on his face.

Coop reached out and shook one of Rocky's hands. "Thanks to you and Shay, I'm going to be fine."

"This here young man's done a fine job, and earned himself a place with the Knitters." Eddy beamed at Rocky, whose chest visibly swelled. "And Shay, it looks like we'll start having to call you the Tenacious Protector again."

I rolled my eyes.

JT raised an eyebrow. "Tenacious Protector?"

Eddy laughed. "I'll fill you in later, JT."

Time for a subject change. "And," I said, "Rocky's going to help out a few days a week at the Hole, since there'll be no more bingo on the barge."

Rocky turned his ten-megawatt smile on me. "Oh yes, Shay O'Hanlon, I am going to help you in your nice coffee shop. Thank you, Shay!"

Tyrell watched the commotion, the lines on his forehead crinkling. "Will someone please tell me what on earth the 'Knitters' are?"

Eddy turned to him, a calculating smile curving her lips. "Let's go and take a walk, you handsome young devil, and I'll tell you all about the Knitters, free of charge." Eddy guided him out of the room.

"Wait for me, Miss Eddy, I want to come! I am going to be a Knitter, too!" Rocky waved at Coop and dashed out the door after Eddy and Tyrell.

Coop's smile faded, and he pinned a dubious gaze on JT. "What's up with Dawg?"

The corners of JT's mouth twitched. "After his observation period and a negative rabies test, he was good to go."

"Where did he go?" Coop frowned.

"You'll see any minute," I told him.

We chatted for a few minutes more, until the door silently swung open again. Dawg burst in the room with a panting Kate in tow. "Sorry, we had to sneak up the stairwell and wait for the all-clear. He looks like a seeing-eye dog to me, but apparently not to anyone else."

JT nudged me and motioned with her head toward the door. Dawg leaped up onto the bed and slurped Coop's face. Kate chattered a mile a minute about the monster-mutt.

We stepped out into the hall. JT grabbed my arm and pulled me through the heavy metal door into the stairwell.

"What—"

My query was cut off as JT pressed me against the wall. The door banged shut. Her eyes were smoking black as she glared at me. "Don't you ever, *ever* do something so stupid again. Trying to handle something like that on your own? You could have gotten Coop killed, not to mention yourself, you silly fool." She stared at me a moment more, and then without warning planted a big smacker right on my lips. Conscious thought evaporated. When she broke away long moments later, we were both panting like *we* were the ones who ran up the steps.

"I've waited forever to do that," she said, resting her forehead on mine, her expressive eyes no longer hard and cold. In fact, they were irresistibly hot, molten.

I smiled at her. "You know, we haven't even had an official date yet, and we're practically making out in the stairwell of a hospital."

"I guess we are," she said.

"So, JT, would you like to go out on a date with me? I know this great little café…"

"A date," JT echoed. "Yes, I'd very much like to have a date with you."

"Glad that's settled. But before we get around to that," I whispered as I pulled her closer to me, my mouth hovering a heartbeat from hers, "I wouldn't mind making out a little more first."

© April McGuire, Back Porch Studios

ABOUT THE AUTHOR

Jessie Chandler, a 17-year bingo hall veteran, State Patrol dispatcher, and former police officer, resides in Minneapolis, Minnesota with her partner, Betty. Boing and Hooch, two frisky felines, graciously allow Jessie and Betty to live with them as long as they behave. As the current vice president of the Twin Cities chapter of Sisters In Crime, Jessie reviews a new mystery for the group every month. When she isn't toiling away at the keyboard or reading her assigned novel, she's schlepping books at Borders Bookshop or leading the LesFic Book Group at True Colors Bookstore. Jessie can also be found hawking artsy T-shirt creations and other trinkets to unsuspecting conference and festival goers during the summer months. Visit Jessie at www.jessiechandler.com and friend her on Facebook at http://www.facebook.com/jchandlerauthor.